**Inspector Proby
in Court**

John Gano
Inspector Proby in Court

This edition published in Great Britain in 1999 by
Allison & Busby Limited
114 New Cavendish Street
London W1M 7FD
http://www.allisonandbusby.ltd.uk

First published 1995 by
Macmillan

A catalogue record for this book is available
from the British Library

ISBN 0 7490 0330 8

Design and cover illustration by Pepe Moll

Printed and bound by Biddles Limited,
Guildford, Surrey.

Chapter 1

It was nearly five o'clock in the afternoon. The windows of the post office in Stockard Street were enjoying their usual quota of autumn sunshine, and Mary Clark, the postmistress, a brisk energetic woman with cheerful blue eyes, was laboriously filling in her day's VAT ledger.

There were only two customers at the front counter, a young woman with frizzy black hair by the window and a short man standing behind her.

The woman was dithering, so Mary dropped her gaze back to the form. 'Fill in box 17 only for input/chargeable variable items.' How was anyone expected to understand their jargon?

'Keep your hands where I can see them.' It was said so softly that if the other customer hadn't screamed, she would hardly have taken it in.

'What…' She was looking straight down the barrel of what looked like a miniature machine-gun.

'Don't try to be a heroine.' She could see him smile under the distorting black stocking stretched over his face. Why were her eyes drawn so insistently to the glimpse of a tattoo on the back of his hand, showing through the polythene glove? 'After all, it's not your money, is it?' There was another taller man in the shop now, bending over the kneeling figure of the young woman. Had they hit the poor creature? Very cautiously and without changing her expression, Mary moved her foot towards the little red button on the floor.

'I can see you're going to be sensible.' His smile was even broader. 'Come over to the door. You're going to lock up early, that's all.' She'd been told there was a fifteen-minute delay on the alarm, to give the police time to get there. She inched her foot nearer, forcing herself to look confused, even idiotic.

'*Come on,*' he said, suddenly apprehensive. 'I haven't got all day.' Mary nodded, and trod on the button. Nothing happened. Relieved, she began to move along the counter. She'd done her bit, now she could co-operate with a clear conscience. 'This won't take long...' Suddenly a screeching metallic wail sounded from just outside in the street.

'The bank!' she said desperately, but the second man had already panicked.

'She's sounded the alarm,' he shouted, clubbing the cowering customer on the floor with the butt of his shotgun.

Mary saw the first man turning towards her, so slowly, and the whole of life seemingly decelerating almost to a standstill. His hood had slipped, revealing a long nose and narrow angry eyes. And yet he was still smiling.

'No, I…' The words wouldn't come. She saw the vicious little muzzle of his gun turning too,

saw his finger tightening and just had time to
think about her children, safe at home with her
sister, when the roaring, flashing, searing explosion flung her body backwards against a filing
cabinet. She heard its loud metallic complaint,
and nothing more.

'Come on, you fool!' Both men ran out into
the street just as the first police car, its headlights
flashing, swerved into view at the top of the street.
Their own car, a bright red Ford Sierra, was
parked by the side of the pavement, neatly
blocked in by a Corporation bus which was
discharging a group of pensioners.

'Hey! What do you think you're doing?' An
elderly builder in dungarees had come round the
corner of the building, followed by another
holding a sledge-hammer. The smiling man
began to fire again.

'Keep your head down!'

Jim Proby, a heavily built man with a shock
of grey hair over a craggy, sunburnt face, was
crouching beneath the parapet, reloading his
revolver, while Detective Sergeant Rootham, his
companion, shorter, fitter, with a neat black
moustache, was peering cautiously across at the
building opposite, another ugly sixties concrete
and glass block. Beneath them yawned a hundred
and fifty feet of plain air down to the evening
traffic halted on the Hampton inner ring road.
Occasionally they could hear the distant sound of

impatient horns muffled by the evening mist already creeping up from the estuary.

'I'm sure they've hopped it by now, sir.' Ted Rootham raised his head and ducked as bullets slammed into the concrete wall behind, scattering the cowering men with chips and dust. The noise of gunfire was deafening. 'Bastard's on the eleventh floor,' he gasped. 'White, thirties.'

'And knows how to shoot!' Proby had finally finished reloading. 'What's he carrying? A Gatling gun?'

'One of those 9 mm Fletcher and Houston jobs from the sound of it. Where do they find these things? The other guy's got a shotgun.'

'I know,' Proby's left hand was speckled with pellet wounds. 'How far across?'

'Sixty, sixty-five feet?'

'Where's Hickock, for Christ's sake?'

'You want to take a look?'

The older policeman grinned. 'How about using the phone?'

On the fourteenth floor of the Gull Insurance building opposite, Detective Constable Hickock was edging his way heavily down the stone staircase when the buzz of his radiophone froze him in mid-step.

'Yes?'

'Where are you?'

'Jesus! They might've heard this.'

'The boss wants to know.'

'Tell him I'm above them. Fourteenth floor. When's the back-up due?'

'I can hear the sirens now. We're coming over.'

'Don't call me, I'll call you,' whispered Hickock with a grim smile. He had just heard the clang of the staircase door some way below him.

There were two of them, two angry ex-soldiers, recently made redundant, with no patience for job centres after fifteen years spent watching their shadows in Ulster and Bosnia. They had been trained to spot a sniper at half a mile, to garrotte a man in ten seconds and to control their grief at the frequent funerals of colleagues. They knew nothing of book-keeping or window-cleaning. But they had taught themselves a thing or two about post offices. This was their third raid in a month. Only this time their driver had let himself get blocked in by the bus.

They came up the staircase one behind the other, the tall one on the inside with the shotgun, while the short one covered their rear, three steps behind him.

Hickock, his massive chest heaving, held his revolver two-handed, the hammer cocked. Was he really going to have to give a warning to these maniacs? Already the postmistress and two pedestrians were dead. What did society expect of its guardians? Sweat was beginning to pour down his face. *Where were they?*

He saw their shadows first, opaque movements on the wall, dimly crosslit by the misty evening sun. This was madness! But it was too late to retreat, too late to hide himself in some reassuring cupboard until the reinforcements came.

'Police!' he heard himself shouting, as the obscene snout of the shotgun inched into view. 'We're armed!"

A man in dirty denims seemed to somersault across the corner step, the flash of his gun preceding a roaring sound as the air whistled with flying metal. Hickock, half-dazed, saw his own shots tearing holes in the man's chest. He never noticed the second man who, smiling broadly, stepped out and emptied a whole magazine of shells into the bulky policeman, continuing to fire long after his victim's face had splintered into spongy oblivion. Without pausing even to examine his companion, he stepped nimbly over Hickock's shattered body, and continued his climb.

'This one's dead too.' Rootham was kneeling by the robber, while Proby, his face in shadow, was gazing down at Hickock. They knew it was him by his clothes, the old patched jacket, the carefully knotted shoelaces, the familiar signs of the difficult but methodical detective to whose widow this dreadful wreck would have to be shown. 'Typical! Four bulls-eyes where one would have done. He knew there were two of them. I bet he even gave them a warning.'

'Come on!' Proby, still out of breath from the climb, took off his coat and laid it over Hickock. 'Who's watching the lifts?'

'Braithwaite and Allan. Oates is out the back and the heavy mob's securing the main stairs. Then they're starting the search.' In the distance they could now hear the clatter of a helicopter. 'We ought to wait.'

If Proby heard him, he gave no sign. Breathing hard, he started to climb the stairs. Rootham stared after him, checked his own gun, and hurried to catch up.

'The roof.'

'Got to be.'

'Right. If he's nimble, he can get across to the Sun Alliance building. I bet that's the plan.' They were running now, two steps at a time, heedless of caution, ignoring the doors at each succeeding floor. At the very top, a steel-grey metal door was marked 'ROOF ONLY – ALARMED'. It was ajar. Rootham tried to elbow his way past the grey-faced Detective Inspector.

'My turn,' he said. He was pushed roughly back.

'I may not have cared for Hickock,' panted Proby angrily, 'but this man answers to me.' He shoved open the door, immediately jumping back in anticipation. Silence. 'Where's that bloody helicopter?'

Rootham handed him the pocket phone which had been buzzing angrily. 'Mr Rankin says to pull back. They're waiting for dogs.'

'What? Hello? HELLO?' Proby had already pushed the aerial back into its socket. 'Useless toys!' he said. 'I couldn't hear a word. Cover me from that window.' He got down on the floor and began to crawl out onto the roof, a jumbled area dangerously crowded with flue pipes and air-conditioning vents. Still silence. There was no parapet. Just a point where the roof ended, and open space began.

'*Help!*'

'Did you hear that?'

The two men listened. Very faintly they heard it again.

'*Help me!*'

Then they saw, on the very edge of the roof, glittering in the sunlight, the stubby silver shape of an automatic pistol, looking quite at home among all the other paraphernalia of modern technology.

'Hang onto my legs, Ted.' Clutching his revolver in one hand, Proby inched his body across the concrete until he reached the edge. Taking a deep breath, he made himself expose his head over the side and looked down. It was all he could do not to cry out. The second robber's head was only a few feet below him, staring up with frightened eyes. He must have slipped trying to secure the cord that dangled away into space from his waist, for he was hanging on to a piece of metal spouting with both hands, his feet flailing in three hundred and twenty feet of empty air above the narrow alleyway separating the two buildings.

'*Please.*' So near and yet so far. The roof of the Sun Alliance building could not be more than twenty feet away, and rather lower. Certainly within swinging distance.

'Give me your hand,' said Proby quietly. The two men stared at each other.

'I can't...' A fellow Yorkshireman!

Proby levered himself further out into space. The helicopter was directly overhead, drowning Rootham's warning shout.

'Give me your hand...' Again the man stared up at him. Proby forced himself to smile. 'Come on, lad.'

With agonizing slowness, the man shifted his grip, his eyes bulging with the effort. Their hands inched together, then met, sweaty but firm. Now Proby had him by his other wrist, transferring the man's weight onto his own shoulders. He could even feel himself sliding forward, drawn over the edge by his burden.

'Hang onto him, somebody!' There were voices behind him. Someone was now helping Rootham with his other leg.

'Have you got him?' No one could hear themselves think with all the swirling dust and the din.

The robber tried to grasp Proby's wrist, but Proby instead twisted his hand until he had the man by both wrists himself. The noise of the helicopter was deafening, a great wind was buffeting them, he felt almost dizzy. With a great effort, Proby braced himself to start pulling the man to safety. And then he saw the man's mouth open into a silent scream, and his face accelerated away, disappearing downwards as the flailing body dropped into space, striking the side of the building and then, finally, scattering some dustbins as it cannoned into the tarmac alley, almost out of sight. Other, whiter faces appeared, staring upwards at the towering roofline. Proby himself being pulled backwards.

'Where is he?' Chief Superintendent Rankin, his hair unusually ruffled by the flailing rotors of the helicopter hovering above them, was shouting against the roar.

'He fell, ' said Proby flatly.

Rankin stared at him for what seemed like an age. 'Too bad,' he said at last. 'Let's go back to the station. We can leave the others to clear up here.'

Chapter 2

'Listen to that helicopter!'

Dr Gresham got up and slammed down the window. A corpulent man, his belly sagging over the snakeskin belt which supported his red cotton trousers, he crossed to the table beside the door and poured himself another glass of ginger-beer. 'Now, about Mrs Bracy?'

'Yes.' The woman sitting opposite him across the broad desk was in her thirties, tall, with a good figure and auburn hair, brushed severely back and secured by a tortoiseshell comb above the nape of her long neck. As Matron of the Hampton Clinic, Barbara Reid was paid thirty thousand pounds a year, and earned it. Inspiring confidence in women, and different, but no less positive, emotions in men, she more than balanced the negative impressions radiated by her gifted, but boorish, employer. Whatever the writing-paper might imply to the contrary, with its impressive list of names, Dr Gresham owned a controlling sixty per cent of the Hampton Clinic and its various associated enterprises. 'There's no problem about the money of course.'

'Of course.' Mrs Bracy, the elderly widow of Hampton's main jeweller, was notoriously rich. 'It's just that...'

'She's off her head?'

Barbara laughed. 'No, that's going too far. But we do have a policy of referring Alzheimer's patients elsewhere.'

'We?'

She shrugged her shoulders. 'You, then. I'm not questioning your judgement...'

'I should hope not.'

'But if we, I mean you, are to be consistent, well, she should be moved.'

'What in particular has set this off?'

'Her rather individual approach to using the washbasin.'

'I see.' He drained his glass and set it down softly. Mrs Bracy was paying an agreeable eight hundred and forty pounds each week for her rose-pink bed-room with matching en-suite bath-room. Her nephew Terence, who now ran the family business, had indicated that she should be kept there as long as possible. With the latest downturn in the economy, fifteen of the Clinic's bedrooms were unoccupied. He had a large mortgage and if it hadn't been for a recent coach crash taking the Hampton branch of the National Art Collections Fund to London, his cashflow would be in even more serious disarray. 'Presumably we don't have to lay on extra-staff for her?'

'Oh no! It's just that...'

'They'd rather be sitting reading the news-paper than cleaning out one old lady's washbasin?'

Again she shrugged. 'They all know the

position,' she said. 'But times will change. And if you've lost good staff, well…' Her voice tailed away. 'Anyway, I thought I should put it to you.'

'And you have,' he said, standing up. 'Thank you. Now, can I offer you a drink?'

She smiled, stood up and shook her head. His determination to seduce this alluring woman was equally matched by her determination to avoid any personal contact with her employer. She liked the job, and she liked the money. She had no intention of jeopardizing either for the dubious pleasure of being bedded by Dr Gresham.

Passing down the corridor, she met a pretty young nurse hurrying in the opposite direction. 'Hello, Hannah,' she said. 'What's the problem?'

The young woman stopped. 'My shift ends in five minutes, Matron,' she replied. 'I'm just getting Colonel Bridgeman his tea.'

Barbara smiled. 'Is he still hiding his whisky under the mattress?'

'Yes, Matron.' They both laughed.

'Well, hurry up, then. It's nearly seven o'clock. He'll be dreadfully thirsty!' The nurse scurried away.

Reaching the door of Room Seventeen, Barbara knocked sharply and walked in. The autumn sun had almost disappeared behind the hill opposite, so that the view through the picture window presented Hampton Cathedral as a mystical vision, a mysterious bulk of spires and pinnacles, with indeterminate rays of angry orange light sparking through the buttresses and back-lighting the central tower, which rose strong and stark above the wooded contour at its back. When had the great central spire fallen? 1346? 1563? It hardly seemed to matter, since no one had ever bothered to replace it.

'Who are you?' A faded voice from the faded bundle of clothes huddled in the bed.

'Hello, Mrs Bracy,' said Barbara cheerfully. 'You've got a lovely view from here tonight.'

'Are you the man from Sotheby's again?' 'No, dear.' Barbara crossed to the bed, and took her patient's wrist. Then she glanced quickly at her chart. Normal. Everything was normal. And might continue so for another twenty years. Poor old woman, and yet she was only seventy-two. 'Do you know where your bell is?'

'The woman looked up at her craftily. 'My bell?'

'Your bell. To summon a nurse.'

'My bell?' She was holding it in her hand, under the sheet.

'Yes, dear.' Barbara pulled back the sheet ruthlessly, and tapped the bell-push. 'This.'

'This?'

'Yes. When you want to go to the toilet, just press the bell. We'll help you get there. We're always ready to help. That's what we're here for.'

The woman nodded blankly.

'Don't forget now, will you, Mrs Bracy?' The

woman stared at her. 'Will you?'

Mrs Bracy shook her head and waited until Barbara had almost shut the door before saying loudly, 'Awful common woman! TOILET indeed!' She threw the bell-push as hard as she could against the opposite wall.

'Are you the Matron?' Barbara had almost collided with a tall fair man, carrying a large bunch of flowers. 'I've come to visit my aunt.'

'Mrs Bracy?'

'Yes.' He looked her up and down. 'I was talking to an admirer of yours the other day.' When she didn't respond, he added, 'Sir Abraham Cassel. He said it was worth getting pneumonia just to be tucked up in bed by you!'

She smiled politely. 'Sir Abraham was an excellent patient.'

'Unlike Aunt Betty?'

Because he had said this in a sympathetic tone, she felt able to acknowledge its truth. 'It's not that she means to be difficult,' she said, adding untruthfully, 'or that we're not all very fond of her – it's just that we're not really equipped or trained to handle her problems.'

'But the good doctor likes the money, eh?' He chuckled away and then suddenly said, 'Would you do me an enormous favour?'

She looked up at him guardedly. Though tall for a woman, her five feet nine felt dwarfed beside his six feet four. 'I really can't promise,' she said.

'As your best client,' he smiled broadly, 'will you accept these flowers from me as a tribute to the pleasure you give?' He tried to present the bouquet with a flourish.

'Certainly not,' she said, almost angry. 'You've brought them for your poor aunt.'

'So I have,' he said, dropping his eyes briefly. 'Ah! Here comes Dr Gresham. I was just enquiring after my aunt.'

'And practising how to present her with flowers, I observe,' added the doctor drily. 'She'll be delighted to see you. Matron, you're wanted in the Dispensary.'

She hurried away, disagreeably conscious that both men were watching her, and wishing she was not wearing such a tight skirt.

Chapter 3

'Have you read the papers?'

Proby was sipping his mid-morning coffee and trying to ignore the sea of documents that had flooded his desk when Rootham put his head round the door with an awkward grin.

'No. Should I?'

Rootham spread a copy of the *Daily Despatch* across all the other sheets. 'Not a good likeness.' Proby stared down at a blurred photograph which showed him glowering from the inside of a moving car. The headline read: 'Summary Justice' with the subheading: '*Inspector acts as Judge, Jury and Executioner?*'

Allan says he reckons that's slander,' said Rootham tentatively.

'Libel,' muttered Proby, engrossed in the text. 'No, they've covered themselves by presenting that as an improbable supposition.' He closed the paper and handed it back. 'Not that I could afford to sue, whatever they bloody say.'

'Mr Rankin says the Chief 's had a rough ride, at the press conference. They wanted to know why you weren't there.'

Proby shrugged. 'Because he told me to stay away,' he said. 'And it's also Police Federation policy. They rang me first thing. Amazing how the grapevine works. You'd think...' The telephone beside him rang and he picked it up. 'Proby... Yes?... Who?... No! I don't give interviews.' He slammed the receiver down. 'Now what about that stabbing. Any sign of Tallentini?'

'None.' Rootham was as relieved as the Detective Inspector at being able to talk about something different, something routine. There wasn't a single person in the building who wasn't speculating about the murderer's abrupt descent, but nor was there anyone who was going to ask Proby himself about it. 'He was spotted at the main rail depot Thursday evening, though no one saw him get on a train. Since then – nothing!'

'And those motorbikes?'

'Poor Hickock was working on that. I've got Braithwaite going through the paperwork now. He was supposed to have today off to visit his girl-friend. I told him there wasn't going to be any overtime payable. That's right?' It was a sore point that the whole of the second floor was having a financial inspection, hence Chief Super-intendent Rankin's arbitrary ban on extra payments until the two dour young accountants from the Audit Commission had ceased combing through the department's worksheets and returned home to Nottingham.

Proby nodded. 'I'm afraid so.'

There was a tap on the door. 'May I come in?' It was the Chief Superintendent, a man whose air of military precision imperfectly disguised an imperial love of luxury.

'Of course, sir.' Both men stood up, noting his gloomy frown.

'"Grace" wants you now, Jim,' he said, carefully closing the door. 'You'd better be prepared for some pretty searching cross-examination.'

'Oh yes?' They none of them had much affection for their immaculate Chief Constable, a man more exercised by his hopes of social success than for police-work in and around the cathedral city of Hampton and known familiarly, but secretly, to his staff as 'Grace Kelly'. 'Why's that then?'

'Because,' said Rankin heavily, 'you dropped a suspect three hundred feet on to some concrete.'

'SUSPECT?' burst out Rootham. 'Did you see what he did?'

'Listen, sonny!' Rankin had taken out a slim Turkish cigarette and screwed it carefully into a short black holder. 'It wouldn't matter two fucks whether he'd dropped the Boston Strangler or Little Bo-Peep. When policemen start dumping people off high-rise blocks, there's a whole industry out there ready and waiting to raise a stink.' He lit the cigarette and blew out a thin spiral of pale blue smoke. 'Geddit?'

Rootham turned away to hide his disgust. The telephone beside Proby rang again. It was Miss Benchley, the Chief Constable's personal assistant. Could he spare five minutes, straight away?

'James!' The Chief Constable had a smooth hard face and a weak mouth. His pale grey hair was slicked back and he was beginning to look like an elderly fashion model. 'How very good of you to come up. Take a seat.' Proby pulled up a steel chair, ignoring the flimsy French armchair that had apparently been set out for him. 'Terrible business.'

Proby nodded. 'I saw Mrs Hickock again this morning.' he said.

The Chief Constable stared blankly, then nodded. 'Dreadful,' he said. 'But the immediate problem is your own little contretemps.' Proby raised his eyebrows. 'I've had Whitehall on the phone all morning. The Home Secretary is very upset.' Again Proby said nothing. 'There'll have to be an inquiry.'

'Does that mean I'll be suspended?'

'Tell me again what happened,' said his superior. 'Just between you and me.' He widened his lips in what might have been intended as an encouraging smile. The inner door of his office was ajar. Was the lumpen secretary taking notes?

Proby leaned back. 'May I smoke, sir?'

The other man's smile faded. 'Go ahead,' he said, reluctantly. 'Use your saucer.' Two cups of anaemic tea had been placed between them.

'Well,' Proby lit a cigarette and laid it across the top of the delicate little cup. 'It's as I said in my report.' This, he noted, lay in solitary prominence on the desk, face up. 'The man…'

'James Creasey.'

'Thank you, sir.' Proby could feel his temper rising. 'Mr Creasey, having murdered Detective Constable Hickock…

'You don't know that,' cut in the Chief Constable. 'Nor is it relevant.'

'No, sir.' It was a fair point. Proby paused for thought. 'I was pursuing the man I now know to be James Creasey as a suspect. He must have slipped while trying to swing across to the Sun Alliance building; I managed to get a grip on him, but he just slithered out of my grasp.' He raised his eyes. The Chief was staring out of the window. Silence fell. The Chief sipped his tea. 'That's it.'

'Did anyone see this?'

The implication was almost more than Proby could take.

'I don't know, sir,' he replied equably. 'Two officers were holding my legs, there was a helicopter overhead. It was getting dark.'

'What about the Sun Alliance offices?' Hadn't he even been to the scene? 'Could anyone have been watching?'

'I doubt it, sir,' said Proby stolidly. 'It has no windows on that side.'

'Really?'

'And, of course, it's quite a bit lower. That's why Mr Creasey was trying to reach it.' Had he gone too far?

But the Chief Constable only nodded. 'I see,' he said. 'I see.' Then, after a reflective pause, 'And you're telling me there was nothing you could do to save him?'

'It's in my report, sir,' said Proby patiently. 'But no, there was nothing I could have done. It was beyond my control.'

When he reached home that evening, there were more than thirty journalists and cameramen, supported by a mobile canteen truck, encamped outside his house.

'Good evening, George,' he said to one, recognizing the local crime reporter from the *Hampton Gazette.*

'Evening, Jim! You've become quite a celebrity: The wiry little man held out his note-book. 'Any comment on the Home Secretary's statement in the Commons?'

Proby shook his head, amid a burst of flash-bulbs. 'No comment,' he said, dredging up a smile. 'You know the rules, lads.'

'This way, Inspector!' He turned and was half-blinded by an adjacent flash. 'One more for our readers.'

He elbowed his way past the microphones and slammed his door shut. Inside, the living-room was in darkness, his wife having long since pulled the curtains against their intrusive visitors.

'Quite a visitation.' She was standing by the kitchen door, her thin lips compressed, her thick fair hair recently washed and hanging loose over her shoulders. He went towards her and held her to him in a long embrace, luxuriating in the feel of her ample body against his. At thirty-nine, she was seventeen years younger than him. Fifteen years of marriage, childless and by no means trouble-free, had in no way dimmed his desire for her, or his need for the comfort of her presence.

'I know,' he said at last. 'I'm sorry.'

'The kettle's on, or would you rather have some whisky?'

'Much rather.' He went over to the fireplace, and sat down on the sofa. Closing his eyes, he listened to her fetching ice from the fridge and the bottle from the far cupboard. What had Mrs Hickock said? Something about 'dying doing what he loved best'? Hickock of all people! No angel, idle even, and not averse to a bribe. But no one deserved such casual destruction. Thank God he didn't have any children either.

'What are you thinking about?' She put the glass on the table beside him. It looked and smelled satisfactorily strong.

He sighed. 'Doug Hickock,' he said.

'When's the funeral?'

He looked up at her. 'Saturday. Only it's to be a cremation.'

'Do you want me to come with you?' She

hated funerals, even missing her own father's.

'No,' he said, drinking deeply and then licking his lips for every vestige of the reviving liquor. 'There's no need.'

'I've taken the telephone off the hook,' she said, kneeling down beside him and caressing his hands. After a few minutes, he began to respond.

Chapter 4

'Miss Reid?'

'Yes, Hannah?' Barbara was sitting at her desk, checking the week's drug-chits. She looked up at the nurse's face and quickly put down her pen. 'Come and sit down, dear.' She crossed to the door of her office and shut it firmly in the face of Mr Judd the Head Porter who was cruising the corridors in search of an audience for his latest story. Then she crossed to the table by the window where she kept an electric kettle and flicked the switch. 'It's milk and one, isn't it?'

The nurse nodded. She was trying not to cry.

'Dr Gresham?'

Another nod. Barbara sighed. There was hardly a nurse in the building who hadn't come to her sooner or later, with tales stretching from lewd suggestions right up to something falling little short of indecent assault. And Hannah, with her creamy complexion and little upturned nose, was just the sort of woman to inflame the Doctor's juices. The trouble was they were all paid well, very well. And there weren't so many jobs about now that Hampton General had cut back on its long-stay patients in favour of the more profitable surgical beds.

'Here's your tea.'

Silent tears were pouring down the nurse's face. 'Thank you,' she mouthed, and sniffed the comforting aroma before delicately sipping the hot liquid. Was she really twenty-three? She looked about seventeen.

'So what happened?'

Hannah shook her head. 'I'm sorry to be so feeble.'

'Tell me what happened,' said Barbara patiently. 'It's much better to talk about it. It's not the first time, I can tell you!' She smiled and was rewarded by an answering gleam.

'I don't want to lose my position.' That's what they all said, and wasn't it true of Barbara herself? Why couldn't the good Doctor find himself a wife and leave them all alone to get on with their jobs? But she knew the answer to that only too well. You only had to spend five minutes in his company to recognize that no sane woman would put up with his oily, patronizing and conceited manner.

'I'm sure there's no question of that,' she replied soothingly. 'Did he touch you?' Silence. 'It really is much better to talk about it. You know that from your training.'

'I was filling the Colonel's hot water bottle.' A tiny disembodied voice. 'He came up behind me. I couldn't do anything because I was afraid of scalding myself.'

'And?'

She had started to cry again. 'He rubbed himself up against me.'

'God!' Barbara sat down heavily. 'What a bastard!' For a few minutes they sat there, the only sound being Hannah's subdued sobs. Then there was a clatter as the girl put the cup firmly down on the table.

'I'm sorry to have burdened you with that,' she said briskly. 'I suppose it's the same everywhere. I must go and check Mr van Oss's blood pressure.' She stood up.

'Why?' said Barbara.

'Why what?' Hannah caught sight of herself in the mirror by the door. 'Oh no! Look at my eyeliner!'

'Why do you suppose it's the same everywhere?'

Hannah shrugged. 'My stepfather. Our headmistress. Life!' She gave a cheery smile. 'Thanks for the tea. I feel so much better, just having a chance to talk about it.' She went out, closing the door softly behind her.

Barbara picked up her telephone and banged it hard on the table. Really, she would have liked to throw it through the window. Seventy-three people worked at the Clinic; thirty-eight full-time, and the rest as casual or contractors. How could you weigh that against a ruthless campaign of sexual harassment, against a man's finger, wander it whithersoever? Gresham up in court, no doubt humiliating Hannah by claiming he had been led on, would put the whole Clinic at risk. And her own mortgage? She got up and stared at herself in the mirror, not from vanity but with a questioning expression.

'What have you become?' she asked the image softly. 'What are you DOING, covering up crime for the sake of peace and quiet?' And yet even that question disgusted her, for she knew she was at least partly guilty of turning away from the truth because of her home, because of the little pink house in Limpsey, with its lavender hedges and the clusters of old roses that had hung over her front door all summer. Compare that to her parents' cramped and evil-smelling flat above the shop in Hounslow and…

There was a tap at the door and the man himself looked in, red in the face and smiling broadly.

'Good morning, Barbara.'

'Good morning, Doctor.' It was occasions like this which made her so grateful that she had always resisted his invitations to call him Peter.

'You're looking rather fierce,' he said, adding, it suits you! I'm about to do my rounds. Anything I ought to know about?'

She forced herself to act naturally. 'No. Everything is normal. There's one new admission, a Mrs Tentercroft. She was referred by the Berington practice, suspected rib fracture. Doctor Singh has examined her and she's due for x-ray at 10 a.m. She's a BUPA Scale A patient, of course.' She handed him the papers.

'Thanks,' he said, and paused in the doorway. 'Remind me, ' he said casually, 'that cheeky nurse with the mole on her neck. What's her name?'

'Hannah Grant,' she said through gritted teeth.

'Of course,' he said, beaming, and walked off whistling, leaving the door ajar.

Chapter 5

The main railway line to London ran south from Hampton, crossing the marshes beside the estuary on a long brick viaduct known as 'The Arches'. One hundred and eighty-three of these spanned the desolate swampland, a haven for wildlife and courting couples, before the track reached the rising ground that, in turn, developed into the Lodden Hills. These, densely wooded at their base, rose fifteen hundred feet up to Lodden Moor, a wide trackless area of scrub and heather, unnoticed by the railway passengers as they were plunged into the sudden mile-long darkness of the Lodden tunnel on their way south.

At noon that morning, two men in overalls were wearily walking down the tracks, occasionally tapping the rails with their steel luggets. All around them the trees flamed with gorgeous autumn colours, reds clashing with copper, yellows with orange. Soon these same leaves would be falling, threatening the line with their acrid debris, the heavily veined foliage piling up thickly against the rails and clogging the wheels as they slithered across the decaying compost. But the two men had no time for the splendours or miseries of nature. Theirs was a prosaic job, to be carried out methodically, regardless of season or landscape.

'Buggers put a sleeper across the line at Claxby last week,' muttered one suddenly.

'No!'

'They did, though. Reg saw it in time. If they'd placed it another few yards up, he'd have run straight into it.' On and on they trudged, the ring of their luggets the only sound apart from the occasional cry of a cock pheasant and once the raucous screech of a jay.

'London train's due.' The older man, whose ruddy face was disfigured by a large hooked nose, shouldered his tool and crossed the two sets of track and clambered down the pebbled embankment. His companion, shorter, wearing a dusty grey cap, followed him, and together they stood, looking at their watches.

'One minute.' Thrillingly, the tracks began first to vibrate and then to hum in an accelerating crescendo. Right on time, a sleek blue-and-white Intercity locomotive with twelve matching carriages backed by its twin dashed round the corner, tore down upon them, its warning shriek almost lost in the din of furiously working machinery, passed them in a tornado of dust and wind, and disappeared behind the trees down the track, leaving them breathless.

'Did Mr Bull say we'd get our tea-break back then, Bill?' The younger man pulled off his cap and scratched his hair.

Bill grunted. 'Come on,' he said. 'The quicker we get this over with the more time we've got to discuss that with the others.' They climbed back onto the track.

A mile further on, just as the trees began to thin out, a series of old points and some earthworks showed where an old branch line had once led east into another part of the forest.

'That's funny.' Bill was staring down the disused line.

'What is?'

'These points here.' He bent down and ran his finger over a bit of rusted metal.

'What about them?'

'They've been greased.'

'Oh, come on.' The other man was bored, and eager for a rest.

'No, look! Here!' He had walked a few yards down the old track. 'There's been a train down here.'

'So what?'

'I don't know,' said his companion, shaking his head, 'but I'm certain it shouldn't have been down there.'

'Tell Mr Bull about it then,' snapped the other, 'but leave it be now. I'm tired, and very hungry.'

By the time they'd reached their depot, Mr Bull the supervisor had gone off shift. A mile across the city, Proby, still smarting from his visit to the

Chief was enjoying the very occasional luxury of
an after-lunch cigarette when Mr Rankin looked
round the door again.

'More bad news, I'm afraid.'

'Oh?'

'I've had a call from a friend of mine in
London. There's going to be a question asked in
Parliament, some rabid Scottish fellow-traveller
of course, but it's rattled the Under Secretary.
And you can imagine the effect that's had
upstairs!' The Chief Constable was a man in
search of a knighthood, and consequently unusually affected by the prevailing mood in Whitehall.

'And?'

'And?' Mr Rankin raised his swirling
eyebrows.

Proby grinned. 'I can tell there's an "and",'
he said.

Mr Rankin shook his head. 'It's no joke,' he
said. 'If the Department of Public Prosecutions
doesn't act, there's talk of a private prosecution
by some bunch of crackpots calling themselves
"Citizens For Safety".'

'Prosecution for what?' demanded
Rootham, who had come in at the tailend of this
conversation.

'Murder,' said Mr Rankin. 'So you'd best be
preparing yourself for a lot of bother.'

Proby stared at him. 'Will they suspend me?'
he said slowly.

'Not while I'm in post.' said Rankin shortly.

'But they'll have to consider it, so for God's sake keep your temper, Jim.'

'Mrs Hickock wants the service at eleven o'clock on Saturday morning.'

'Good. Who's doing the arrangements?'

'I am.'

'Do you want the band?'

'I've booked them already.'

'Cathedral?'

I've got to see the Dean at three.'

'Told the Chief?'

Proby paused. 'I was hoping you'd do that.'

'Ta, very much!' Rankin turned his mouth down. 'In that case I'll get it over with. Pass me that phone. He stabbed at the dial and waited. 'Rankin here,' he said after a pause. 'Yes, please.' Another pause. 'Rankin here,' he said again. 'I thought you'd want to know Hickock's funeral will be at eleven o'clock on Saturday, sir.'

As he listened he began to turn red. It started with his neck, but the colour crept up his face like a waterline, until his inflamed scalp showed through the patches of scrubby grey hair. 'It is normal to follow the family's wishes, sir. Yes. Yes, it is most unfortunate. No, sir. I don't think you can do that... because...' He put his hand over the mouthpiece. 'He's shooting at Lodsworth Castle. Can we make it Monday?' The other two stared at each other in disgust. 'No, sir. I'm afraid Mrs Hickock was absolutely adamant.' He held the receiver away from his ear and pulled a comic face, miming the chattering of the buck-toothed old crone. 'Thank you, sir. I'm sure that's for the best.'

'Christ!' he said, and walked out of the room.

It was just past three o'clock when Proby parked his red Saab on the cobbles outside the Deanery, a handsome redbrick house, with tall Georgian windows overlooking the Cathedral's west door. There was a queue of people standing on the wide steps opposite, waiting perhaps for the Cathedral's controversial new turnstile recently installed to regulate the flow of tourists. There had been questions in Parliament about that too. Altogether they seemed an inquisitive lot.

He rang the bell and immediately the door was flung open. 'Inspector Proby?' The Dean was a short round man, with a creased face and long side-whiskers 'This is a very sad occasion.'

Proby followed him through a high hallway into a small room hung with ecclesiastical portraits and warmed by a flaring gas fire of imitation logs. A very fat spaniel made a half-hearted effort to get up.

'Stay!' Was this the tone he used with recalcitrant canons? 'Now,' he was watching Proby with a guarded expression. 'Tell me what you want.'

'Well,' Proby sat down on the nearest chair, a spreading swollen creation in a faded green cotton material covered with dog hairs. 'It's really what Mrs Hickock wants.'

'Indeed.' The Dean rubbed his hands, and held them up to the fire.

'A couple of hymns, two or three prayers. She was very anxious about keeping to the 1662 prayerbook.'

'Indeed?' The Dean's smile broadened. 'Just what I would have suggested myself.'

'She wants the Assistant Chief Constable to give the address.'

'Not Richard Mason?' Proby was so unused to the Chief Constable's name that for a moment he was nonplussed. 'No problems so far,' added his host.

'Any preference for hymns?'

Proby shifted awkwardly, and produced a small piece of paper. '"O God, our help in ages past,"' he read out loud. 'And "There is a green hill far away."'

'Charming,' said the Dean. 'Charming.'

'We do appreciate your co-operation,' said Proby after blowing his nose into his freshly ironed handkerchief. 'It makes such a difference to all of us.'

The Dean raised one hand. 'I assure you,' he said, 'it's the other way round. We are conscious of being a highly visible part of Hampton. Sometimes I fear people see us as being more decorative than practical. When the community suffers a tragedy like this, we so want to be SEEN to be active in playing our role.'

'As to costs…?' Proby looked at his feet.

'Don't even think about it, my dear fellow. We do indeed exact our ounce of flesh, or do I mean our widow's mite,' he paused to chuckle, 'from the general public; but from our friends the police…' He waved his hands airily. 'Not one penny!'

'Thank you very much.' Proby was trying to seek an excuse to leave.

'One thing.' The Dean's eyes glittered. 'The Bishop did mention to me this morning that he wondered whether an opportunity might be found, tactfully, to express some sort of, er, *Christian* forgiveness for the man who fell, and indeed his friend.' Proby held his expression rigidly in place. 'He thought some little mention of them might not go amiss, something along the lines of "fellow sufferers"? I should so like to hear what you think, Inspector.'

Proby adopted his most professional air of calm. 'I don't think that would necessarily achieve the end the Bishop has in mind,' he said, summoning up a conspiratorial half-smile. Not unless the Bishop was after promoting a riot! 'It's a very magnanimous thought, but given the composition of the congregation, and especially Mr Hickock's family, I would have suggested a separate occasion of the Bishop's own choosing. No doubt his sentiments would be as spiritually efficacious even if expressed modestly, in private?'

The Dean sat back and folded his hands slowly. 'Very tactfully put, Inspector,' he said at last. 'Are you by any chance of the Roman persuasion?'

'No,' said Proby. 'My wife and I are members of the Graceby congregation.'

'The perpendicular splendours of All Saints.'

'Yes.'

'Under my old friend the excellent Dr Phillips?'

'Yes.'

'Well, well! Anyway, I will tell Bishop Barry what you have said. Incidentally,' the Dean added almost as an afterthought, 'would I be right in thinking it was you who so nearly managed to save the man Creasey?'

'Yes,' said Proby. 'You would.'

The Dean's eyes positively flashed. 'So nice to have met you, Inspector.' He held out his hand. As Proby walked through his front door, he called after him 'Oh, Inspector!'

'Yes?'

'The Church of England will hear confessions for those who seek solace, you know.'

Proby turned on his heel. 'I'll bear it in mind,' he said with a smile. And he was amazed to find himself laughing aloud as he let himself into his car.

Chapter 6

'Bloody old bat!'

'Who?' Hannah's nursing duties started early on a Saturday morning because she had a regular lunch-time date with her married sister who worked in the City Centre.

'Mrs Barmy Bracy, that's who,' said Mr Judd, the Head Porter who was trying to complete his overtime roster and eat a piece of burnt toast at the same time. 'Pretends she's up in the clouds one minute, and then there she bloody is, spying on you the next.'

'What's she caught you at now?' laughed Hannah, drying the last cup and saucer from the previous evening's cocoa round.

'It's not funny,' the old man grumbled. He hadn't shaved yet, and a thick white stubble blurred his normally shining red cheeks. 'The patients expect a little pampering.'

'Colonel Bridgeman's bottle?'

He winked at her. 'A fine gentleman,' he said. 'Pays on the nail, and always a bit extra for me. "There you are, Judd," he says, like I was some effing stage butler. Some people!' His last piece of toast shattered into a mass of black crumbs and he swore loudly.

'Look at the time!' murmured Hannah tactfully. 'Matron'll be along in a moment. I must go and brush my hair.'

All over the city, the first rays of a rosy dawn were creeping across the roofs, sending tendrils of light along the cracks in the sleepers' curtains, and painting delicate pink and blue mosaics on the cold Cathedral floor. Proby, lying awake on his back, was listening to his wife's regular breathing, grateful for the warm pale arm she had suddenly flung across him, whimpering in her sleep and then mouthing some incomprehensible jumble of sounds. Could he have saved the man? Had he deliberately meant him to fall? The thoughts and memories all blurred together. In the far distance, he could now hear the muffled clatter of the first train crossing 'The Arches' on its way south. That sound meant there was a frost, or that the wind was in the west, blowing the cold Atlantic air up the estuary, either way chilling his uniformed colleagues out on their beats, alone or in pairs, trying to deter crime and keep the citizens of Hampton secure in their homes.

The Chief Constable was also awake, standing by his bedroom window, staring mournfully out across the ploughland that separated his converted barn from the banks of the estuary. His wife, a doughty little woman three years older than him with a hard rock-like face, was already downstairs raking out the wood-burning stove. This was the day she should have been laying out his smart new Huntsman suit of jacket, waistcoat and knee-breeches in green and grey tweed discreetly mixed with a reddish twill. He should have been unlocking his gun cabinet, and fitting together the lovingly oiled Holland and Holland shotgun with its engravings of flying birds. He should even, and this was the bitterest thought, have been spending his first day's shooting as a guest of Lord Lodden, enjoying the easy camaraderie of Lord Lodden's guests from London. Instead he was having to go to a service in a Cathedral, and maybe even attend a cremation!

'No!'

'What is it, Richard dear?' His wife bustled in, carrying his cup of tea, complete with two shortbread biscuits balanced on the saucer.

'I absolutely refuse to go to a cremation.'

'Quite right, dear.' His wife had learnt that the secret of getting her own way in everything was never to oppose her husband in anything outside her own immediate interests.

'But HOW can I get out of it? Apparently I'm almost the only non-family person to be invited.' His wife paused to think. Nothing disturbed the even tenor of her mind, so after a decent pause, she went silently back downstairs.

The post office that had been the subject of the violent attack was in Stockard Street, and the Incident Room following the crime was set up in the police station just across the green in Jewgate. Both gunmen were dead, but their driver was presumably still alive. He had vanished in the confusion during which the two bystanders had been shot. 'Thirties, white, blue jeans, a beard' was, in its own way, not a bad basis for a search, given that both his accomplices proved to have been recently discharged from the Forty-Ninth Fusiliers, a regiment whose main recruiting area bordered Hampton. There was also one witness who thought he might have been caught by a ricochet in the leg.

Under Proby, as Senior Investigating Officer, a busy office of fifteen people working alternate twelve-hour shifts, continued to try to piece together the events leading up to the tragedy, as well as leading the hunt for the missing fugitive.

The crime being a Category A offence (of grave public concern) Proby had initially been allocated a force of thirty-six detectives together with twenty-eight uniformed men for the street-by-street enquiries around Hampton. By eight that morning, he was already sifting through the interim analyses prepared by Mrs Sentance who had doubled as Receiver and Statement Reader for the night shift.

There had been three suspected sightings of the fugitive, one as near as Berington Junction, and the shotgun had been positively identified as one of two stolen from a gun club's premises in Huddersfield.

'Nothing on the machine-gun?'

Mrs Sentance, a tall thin woman with heavy black spectacles, shook her head. 'There was a call from Mr Jenkins, Regional Crime Squad. One of their targets used one in the Brighton area,' she said.

'You've got all this on the computer?'

She gestured at the two indexers busily bent over their modems at the back of the room. The whole room stank of hot machines and cold pizzas. 'What time are you going up to the Cathedral?'

He looked at his watch. 'The procession leaves Brigstocke Street at 10.40. I'm meeting them on the steps at 10.55. I think I'll walk. Have you fixed my appointment with Major Sitwell?'

She nodded. 'And I've prepared you an itinerary,' she said, with a slight smile. Proby's lack of map sense was all too well known. 'Now, here's yesterday's timesheets. You'll have to initial them for those bastards from Nottingham.'

At a quarter to eleven, he strode out of the long low police station, turned left up Jewgate and began the long climb up the Wynde, a narrow medieval path that meandered precipitously between the heavy stone relics of Hampton's pre-industrial past.

A trading centre since Roman times, the old buildings had seen many changes. Originally stores combined with the merchants' homes, many of them were now converted into flats, with offices or bric-à-brac shops at street level. Occasionally intrusive redbrick blocks showed where persistent wartime bombing of the docks had struck further east, shattering the carefully evolved tapestry of a thousand years of architecture. The planners of post-war Hampton had seen no virtue in restoring its homogeneity; there was even a heavy essay in Bauhaus maroon brick named after their German twinned town, a living affront to those who still resented the violent evidence of earlier European interventionism.

'You did a good job the other day.'

He turned to see who had spoken, finding himself facing a short spare man with a sunburnt face.

'It's Tom Hall, isn't it?' He'd last seen him in the dock up at the Assize Courts, going down for six years for burglary, aggravated by the indiscriminate use of a crowbar.

'Drop the buggers! That's what I say.'

'When did you get out, Tom?' It was Proby's evidence that had put him away.

'Last November. Good behaviour! I can't stick villains who use guns. Gives us all a bad name. You drop a few more. Keep up the good work!' The man gave a cheery wave and continued on down the hill. Proby trudged on. Everyone seemed to assume he'd let the man fall on purpose. And now he couldn't even be sure himself!

At last he reached the old Roman archway that led into the Close. There was a small crowd behind the barriers, mostly officers' wives, some of whom he recognized. There were also two television teams and a familiar bevy of photographers, some of whom greeted him with an explosion of flashbulbs. Feigning indifference, he went over to the Dean who was talking to two other clergymen.

'All in order, Inspector?'

'I believe so.' The cortège had left on time, and indeed within a short while, they could hear the wail of the sirens. Twenty uniformed constables took up their positions lining the steps, just as the motorcycle outriders swept into the Close, followed by the lumbering hearse and three Police cars, the first flying the Chief Constable's flag.

He hurried into the Cathedral, only dimly conscious of its soaring roof supported by the richly carved pillars. Around two hundred people were already seated in the choir, and he could see the Bishop standing awkwardly in a side aisle, adjusting his mitre before a mirror held up by a sweating verger. Hickock! Of all the men on his team, the one least likely to appreciate all this pomp. 'The pall-bearers have got a job on!' he thought, and instantly felt ashamed. Hickock's bulk hadn't made him more or less fit for such a savage death.

'Douglas Hickock was a man who offered everything he had in the service of our community, and who, in the end, was asked to lay down his very life, everything indeed, in the course of his duty as a gallant policeman. How many of us reflect enough on the supreme sacrifice, the threat of which accompanies each of these public servants, as his or her constant companion out there on our streets?' The Assistant Chief Constable, resplendent in the uniform he rarely left his house without, had overall responsibility for operational policing, hence his role now in giving the address. Ten feet from the ornate wooden pulpit, Hickock's body lay encased in a coffin hidden beneath the County Constabulary's flag which was midnight blue and embellished with a large red-and-gold crown topping the county logo. 'Our deepest sympathy goes out to his widow... er... Beryl,' he leaned over the pulpit and directed a blazingly insincere smirk towards the grim-faced woman who was glowering up at him from beside a man who must, by resemblance, have been her brother.

'...His life cruelly cut short in its very prime...' Would he never stop? Proby began to glance anxiously at his watch. The man had been speaking for more than twenty minutes. The Chief Constable looked as if he was ready to walk out. Even the Dean, splendidly installed under a richly carved canopy opposite the Bishop, was beginning to flag.

And suddenly it was over. A short last hymn, stridently accompanied by the police band, then the coffin was shouldered manfully by Rootham, Oates, Allan, Braithwaite, and two others from Records where Hickock had served a brief period in exile, and out they marched, followed by the steady tramp of an obedient congregation retreating under expert orders.

Outside, a steady drizzle had driven away the television teams, and Proby could see the Chief Constable having some sort of argument with Mr Rankin which ended in the former climbing angrily into his car, ready to follow the hearse on its slow journey back down the hill. Turning his back on them all, he walked quickly back down the Wynde to where he had parked his car in the station compound. Ten minutes later, he was speeding down the Castlewick road with Rootham beside him, bound for the army barracks eighty miles east in Doverthorpe.

Chapter 7

Unerringly guided by Mrs Sentance's map as interpreted by Rootham, Proby pulled up at the red-and-white striped barrier outside the Prince Arthur Barracks at Doverthorpe, a good ten minutes before his appointment. There were rolls of razor-wire on either side of the bollards, and a machine-gun emplacement where the ground rose to their left. From the right, two soldiers with weapons slung at the ready approached them warily.

'Detective Inspector Proby?'

'That's me, with Detective Sergeant Rootham.'

'May I see your pass, sir?' The Corporal was firm, but polite. The other soldier was already running a wheeled mirror under the car's chassis.

'CO's not back from an exercise yet. The Adjutant said would you mind waiting in the Officers' Mess. Through the gates, first left and park by the cannon.'

'Fine by me.' Proby took back his identity pass and folded it carefully away, before winding up his window and driving slowly into the military base. So this was where they had trained. Maybe the corporal had even been their friend. They must have all been about the same age. The barracks was a series of three-storey brick blocks, eighteenth-century by the look of them, that stretched away in ordered ranks, three abreast, bounded on one side by the bank of a canal. They followed the tarmac road round onto a parade ground, dominated by a titanic cannon, jet black and mounted on massive wooden blocks.

'Eyes… *Right!*' A group of men, perhaps forty, were being put through a complicated marching manoeuvre, and the air resounded to the tramp of their feet, and the harsh strangulated cries of their drill-master. Behind them, a low modern building spread out at right angles to the last barrack, the sodden regimental flag dangling listlessly from its crisp white pole.

'The Officers' Mess, I presume,' murmured Proby. 'Hope they let you in, Ted!'

Rootham grinned. 'If they don't,' he said, 'I reckon I'll nip round to the Sergeants' Mess. I'd probably learn a sight more there anyway.'

'Maybe so, but I need you to take notes.' They walked up the steps of the Officers' Mess to be met by a young man in a white drill jacket, just as the distant rumble of a drum and braying of trumpets announced the approach of a military band.

'Welcome, gentlemen,' said the steward with an all-embracing smile. 'I have coffee or tea at the ready. Or something stronger, maybe? Come right inside.' They looked at each other, and followed him into a long comfortable room furnished with a number of small tables with easy chairs round the outside. A vast dining-table occupied the centre of the room with a solid majesty, much assisted by its sparkling array of polished silver trophies. Tall portraits of fighting men in festive uniforms hung along the walls. None were smiling, choosing instead to present faces of solemn menace, at odds with their brilliant attire.

'That's our present Colonel,' said the orderly, pointing to a smaller canvas on the end wall, depicting an elderly man in a similar scarlet dress uniform, but without the heavy display of military medals worn by the others. Instead, one large silver decoration adorned a violet sash slashed diagonally across his chest.

'I'll go for coffee, please,' said Rootham.

'And you, sir?'

'The same.'

'Sandwiches?'

It was only then that Proby realized they'd had no lunch. 'Yes please,' he said. 'Anything you've got.'

They were still munching the delicate chicken and mayonnaise offerings and listening to the military music outside, when a middle-aged man in battle-dress hurried in.

'I'm so sorry,' he said. 'Tracks came off one of our vehicles again. I'm Frank Sitwell. You must be Inspector Proby?' They all shook hands. 'I

know why you're here of course. Creasey and
Gilbert?' Proby nodded. 'Great shame for the
Regiment. Creasey particularly. He was my
Sergeant on my first tour in Londonderry. A
good man in a scrap.' Rootham took out his note-
book. 'Any more on the missing man?'

'We were hoping you might help us identify
him.'

The Major narrowed his eyes. 'Well, of
course I'd like to try.' He sounded rather half-
hearted. 'Any real reason to think he might be
one of ours too?'

Proby poured himself another cup of coffee
from the Regimental pot. 'Two witnesses spoke of
a tattoo.' It was a lie but not unreasonable, given
the tattoos on the other two.

'And?'

'A seahorse, on the back of his left hand.'

'I *see*.'

'Many of your soldiers have that... the
Corporal who let us in, the orderly who brought
us the coffee...'

'Yes, yes.' The Major spread out white
unadorned hands. 'What can I say? I'm afraid we
must assume the third member of the gang was
also a Fusilier. What other description have you?'

Rootham consulted another notebook.
'Large, stocky, staring eyes, darkish beard, late
thirties, bit of a belly on him.'

The Major stroked his chin. 'The beard of
course would have come after leaving us.'

'Were Creasey and the other dead man, Gilbert, particularly close?' asked Proby thoughtfully.

'Yes,' said the Major promptly. 'They were always good mates. I remember in Dubrovnik, when we had to evacuate those Pakistani women, they were the two who cleaned out a nest of snipers. Gilbert was the best engineer I ever had. He could fashion a field-gun out of a couple of old bicycles.'

'Were they friendly with anyone else?' Very casually put.

The Major's face was a study in concentration. 'No,' he said at last. 'No one in particular.'

'And they left the regiment… how?'

This time Sitwell positively winced with remembered pain. 'Bloody politicians,' he said. 'Every budget-holder to rationalize his personnel by eleven per cent. Rationalize! I'd like to bloody rationalize a few in Westminster, starting at the top!' He laughed apologetically. 'I'm sorry,' he said, 'but how do you "rationalize" men who've maybe saved your life?'

'No question of dishonourable discharge, anything like that?' asked Proby. He could see he was getting nowhere. 'No? Well, we must be getting back. It was worth a try. We don't want any more people getting hurt.'

'Or dropping off the tops of buildings, I imagine?' The Major's face held a bland smile as he spoke, at odds with his tone. And, when the orderly joined him on the steps as the two policemen drove away past the cannon, he added, 'Good luck, Jack Holland, wherever you are.'

At British Rail's Maintenance Depot, a collection of Second World War Nissen huts behind the marshalling yard, the Deputy Area Supervisor had also lunched on sandwiches, although his were yesterday's fare, the relics from 'The Traveller's Bar' that his wife and sister-in-law managed on Platform One of the mainline station. He could always gauge the popularity of their new lines in fillings. For eight days now he had had nothing but Tandoori Corned Beef, whereas it was over a year since he had last enjoyed his favourite Cheese 'n' Tomato.

He was just carefully disposing of the last one into the refuse bin when there was a tap at the door, and Mr Bull, his Assistant (Tracks and Sleepers, Mainline) poked his domed head round the lintel.

'Yes, mate?'

'I've brought Bill Evans to see you. He's got some cock-and-bull story about someone using one of the old branch lines.'

'Oh yes?' The Deputy Area Supervisor yawned. 'Well, shunt him in then.' The older tracksman shuffled in through the door and stood awkwardly before the summit of his particular professional pyramid. People talked of an Area Supervisor, and sometimes, late at night, when the canteen fire was dying down, there were even whispers of a Regional Manager, a monster of mythic legend. But this man was epic, enough for him, holding as he did the power of job or dole over every living creature this side of the Dimcester road. 'Well then?'

'It was like this,' said the unhappy Bill, going on to explain how he had found the points newly greased.

'And which points were those?'

'Just past the old five mile signstone.'

'Going which way?'

The man stared awkwardly. 'Which way?'

'North or south of the signstone?'

He paused to think. 'South,' he said, 'I think.'

The Supervisor reluctantly rose from his chair and crossed to a large framed map on the wall opposite the window. He stared at it for a while and then jabbed at it with his finger. 'There?'

The tracksman shambled over and stared. 'Yes,' he said. 'I reckon that's exactly it.'

'Well, no one'd want to use that track!' said his superior in disgust. That's the old Lodsworth Castle coal line. Goes straight through the park and into the castle cellars. Fat lot of good that'd be!'

'Don't you think we ought to check it out?' asked Bull, a methodical man for all his wild white brush of hair.

'No,' sighed the Supervisor. 'I don't.' The delicious drowsiness of the afternoon was already stealing over him, bringing to his limbs the same sense of autumnal lassitude that affected the broad quiet woods that covered the hills on all sides of Hampton.

Across the whole city, from a hundred different bonfires, the nostalgic smell of burning leaves began to spread. In the parks, in the gardens, in the school playgrounds, and even in the grounds of the Hampton Clinic, people were hard at work, with rakes, and boards, and wheel-barrows, gathering up the season's first harvest of decay. And, as these aromatic spirals ascended into the damp afternoon air, another spiral joined them, the no less acrid smoke from the Crematorium chimney, the implacable incense of Constable Hickock's funeral pyre.

Chapter 8

'You made a real mess of it!' The speaker was standing in a tall stone building whose walls were honeycombed with strange square box-shaped compartments. He was looking down at a bearded man lying weakly on a pile of old sacking.

'Eff off!' The bearded man turned his face away. 'They're both dead, aren't they? It was nothing to do with me.'

'I've brought you some stew and a baked potato.'

'Great! Now what about my leg?'

'I've told you before,' said the other patiently. 'It'll heal. I daren't let a doctor see you. You've just got to lay up here until you can walk.'

'It's bloody freezing here at night,' protested the bearded man.

'You must be used to that. Don't whine.'

'You wouldn't speak like that if Jim Creasey were here.'

'Well, he isn't, is he, so shut up, and be grateful I took you in.'

'You didn't have much choice, I reckon,' said the bearded man slyly.

The other looked at him speculatively. 'I suppose I could have killed you,' he said coldly. 'Maybe I still will. But I prefer to think we still have a continuing partnership. Did you read any of the books I brought you?'

'Not likely. Load of rubbish! I'd like a newspaper though.'

'I'll take them back then.' He scooped up a small pile of hardback books. 'I'll see about getting a paper tomorrow.'

'And make it a proper one, none of that serious junk.'

'If you don't behave, I'll bring you the Guardian,*' laughed his tormentor. 'I've put a clean bucket in the corner for you.'*

'Makes a change, having the screw doing the slopping out!' said the bearded man, but his voice held too much rancour to amuse his companion. After the latter had left, the bearded man heard him turning a heavy key in the lock. With a sigh, he turned over, cradling his left leg as he did so, and tried to go back to sleep.

For Proby, Sunday morning normally meant an hour's extra sleep, and a long lazy period in bed, reading the newspapers, with his drowsy wife's warm body wrapped against his, her head resting quietly on his chest. But for once, she was up before him, the noise of the shower filtering through the haze of last night's alcohol. They had shared a bottle of Lebanese wine, and had made the mistake of broaching a second, gifts from Mr Rankin. He groaned aloud, and then, sitting up, he swung his legs out of bed and stumbled to the washbasin.

'God!' He stared at the image before him in the mirror: the rumpled face, blurred by silver stubble, the bloodshot eyes, the blotched cheeks. Mid-fifties? Mid-seventies more like! And yet, despite the hangover, he felt no older than when he had pushed Sheila, a young widow and suspect in her own husband's murder case, down onto the chaise longue in that ritzy King's Road flat and taken her with such frantic haste that it was only afterwards that he realized how enthusiastic she too had been. And now? Ruefully he began to shave, scraping away the night's new growth, restoring a semblance of respectability to the tramp who mocked him in the mirror with such a satirical smile.

'I've made your toast.'

Sheila Proby, swathed in a scarlet silk wrap, damp blonde hair everywhere, was standing in the doorway. How many lovers was it? Five, six? He couldn't blame her. She was so vivid, so alive, whereas sometimes he…

'Come on!' she said. 'I want to talk to you.'

Was it so wrong that he loved her, not despite her indiscretions, but perhaps even more, because of them? Didn't she always come back, always show him a love which, if not exclusive, was certainly warm and intense? He rubbed at his hair with the towel, and then followed her down the narrow staircase.

A plate of buttery toast, a pot of her own marmalade and a fresh jug of coffee welcomed him to the table.

'What do you think about adopting a child?'

She was now standing with her back to him, watching the yellowing leaves drifting down from the alder tree in their garden.

'A child!' It was his fault, or so the doctor said, that, in fifteen years, she had never conceived. He stared at her, startled by the unexpected idea.

'Yes!' She turned back to him, her eyes dark with the intensity of her thoughts. 'Yes!'

'Are you sure…?' His voice tailed away. At his age? And she would be forty next March. She scarcely looked twenty-five. 'Someone else's?'

'Yes.' She was nodding forcefully, her pale face suffused with colour. She was blushing! 'It would make such a difference, don't you feel that too?'

'Well… yes.' What else could he say? 'How do we go about it?' He drank some of the scalding coffee, spooning in more sugar, more for something to do than for its sweetness.

'That's easy,' she said, laughing now. 'I've been in touch with the Adoption Society, and with Social Services. They want us to make an appointment.'

'I see.' No wonder she hadn't been able to sleep.

'Look!' She brought out a large glossy leaflet, and opened it at a page with its corner turned down. 'What about Debbie? I think she looks sweet.'

Proby took the paper, and looked at the

wistful little girl staring at him from the photograph. Why was he reminded of that puppy in the petshop window in Ripon, all those years ago? 'Debbie,' he read, 'born 19 February 1986.' That made her eight.

> 'A very friendly, outgoing girl who loves a cuddle. She sometimes lacks confidence and acts younger than her years. As a result of some difficult early experiences, Debbie takes time to trust men, but her social worker believes there is a lot of hope for her, providing she can find a family who can accept some rather trying behaviour until she settles down. She wants a "forever" family, and has been waiting for one for a long time.'

'Poor kid.' He sighed and handed it back. He'd saved up for three months for that puppy. And then it had run away the first day.

'Or we could adopt a baby, if you'd rather? You don't mind, do you?' She came over and sat on his lap. Enfolding him in her long white arms. She smelt of, what – coconut and something indefinable, perhaps even milk?

'No, darling.' But a child! He was due to retire in four years' time. The mortgage was nearly all paid off, but his pension would not be generous. Even so, why not? He felt himself smiling, carried along by her infectious mood.

'It's a lovely idea.'

'You're not angry?'

'Of course not.'

She kissed him hard on the mouth, hugging him fiercely. It was only after a minute or so that he felt her face growing hotter, and the trickle of tears running down from her cheek to his.

Once he reached the Incident Room, he put all thoughts of his future family aside. An identical submachine-gun had been recovered the night before, after an abortive bank-raid in Bristol. Fletcher and Houston were a specialist armourers manufacturing under licence to NATO. Their factory, in Lincolnshire, was a model of security, and none of their clients had ever reported the loss of their devastating merchandise, restricted as they were to a dozen favoured military units. Certainly none had ever been issued to the Forty-Ninth Fusiliers.

'The Assistant Chief Constable nearly had a fit when he saw those overtime chits,' murmured Mrs Sentance when she brought him his coffee.

'What does he expect? You can't run a major investigation on office hours. Whatever anyone says.'

'I'm just warning you.' She slipped away to answer one of the row of telephones on the central table.

A child! A baby! He had no idea how to change a nappy. Outside, the telephone wires across the Green were thronged with small birds, row upon row of them, while little flocks eddied in the breeze. Where were they going? Did they really cross the sea, lured south by some strange hereditary knowledge of warmer climates, or were they, like Columbus, driven by the search for adventure, already bored by their short summer's life? He sighed. A week or two in the sun wouldn't be unwelcome to the Probys, away from Assistant Chief Constables and those sharp-suited young men from the Audit Commission.

'Anything new?' It was Rootham now, poking his head round the door with a cheery smile.

'You're supposed to be at home.' Rootham had a mousy little wife and twin daughters, budding ballet-stars and all of ten years old.

'Did you hear about the rail-crash?' Proby shook his head. 'It was on Radio Hampton just now. No one hurt.'

'That's all right then.' Proby accepted the proffered cigarette. 'Tomorrow, we'll check out this gun factory. It's not such a long drive.'

Chapter 9

'I saw you.' The voice from the bed was so faint that for a moment Hannah thought she had imagined it.

'I'm sorry?'

Mrs Bracy's eyes sparkled in the doughy desert of her face. 'I saw you, you little slut.'

Hannah stopped shaking the thermometer and looked down at her patient. 'I don't understand,' she said after a pause.

'Yes you do,' said the other softly. 'You think I'm trapped here, helpless. But I'm not.' Suddenly, shockingly, she sat up energetically, her nightdress falling off one shoulder. 'Though how you could do it is past me. Little Goody Two-Shoes! Gorging yourself on that old man. Rather you than me. I hope he's paying you well.' She chuckled as the little nurse ran out of the room, the smashed thermometer lying where it had fallen on the linoleum. 'That'll teach her.' Suddenly exhausted, she lay back on her pillows, and began to snore.

'What is the matter? Hannah! Stop this.' Barbara had found the young woman sobbing in the Dispensary, her body hunched over the counter, her face hidden between clenched fists. 'What *is* the matter? What's he done now? It's Dr

Gresham, isn't it?'

Hannah shook her head vigorously. 'Please tell me.' Again a shake of the head. 'How can I help you if you won't explain?'

'I can't.' Hardly audible.

'Of course you can.'

Hannah sat up, pulled out her handkerchief and rubbed her face hard. 'I'd like to give in my notice, Matron. As from now. I'm going to collect my things.'

'But Hannah! You can't. I need you. You know that.'

'I can't help that.' Her face was set in a blank mask, eyes fixed on the floor, yet her mouth was still quivering.

'Is it something I've done?'

'Oh no, Matron.'

'Or said?'

'You've been so kind to me.'

'Then you can tell me, can't you?' Barbara shut the door, and let her hand rest tremulously on the nurse's shoulder.

'Mrs Bracy.'

'Mrs Bracy? Oh no! Don't tell me she's been sick again. I told her not to keep having the blancmange.' Hannah gave a little giggle. 'There now, you can tell me.'

'She saw me.'

'Saw what?'

The little nurse turned her tragic eyes to the older woman's face and stared, as if to gauge whether she could really confide in her. Barbara stared back, trying to hide a growing professional unease. After all, what had the nurse done that shouldn't have been seen? Drugs? It was an occupational temptation, no different from the lure of alcohol to a publican.

'I know I shouldn't have.'

Barbara put her arm firmly round the girl's shoulders. 'What?'

'The Colonel.'

'The Colonel!' Was it only a matter of a little whisky?

'He offered me a hundred pounds.'

'For WHISKY?' The poor man must have been desperate.

'No.' Just a whisper, yet its tone explained everything, or nearly everything.

'Oh,' Barbara hugged her tighter. 'Well.'

'Are you very shocked?'

'No, dear. I expect you made him very happy.'

'Oh yes.' Hannah giggled. 'He's offered double for, well for a bit more.' Barbara took away her arm. 'Of course I said no.' She gazed anxiously up at the Matron. 'I don't know how that old cow could have seen. We had the door closed.'

'Naturally.'

'You want me out now, don't you?'

Barbara stared at her, at the dark defiant eyes, the rosebud lips, the perfect complexion of a healthy young animal, bartered to a lonely old man, though perhaps more out of affectionate pity than simple greed. 'No,' she said, making herself smile. 'Of course I don't. But...'

'But?'

'But... I don't think we should let Dr Gresham hear of it.' The young nurse's mouth twisted into an expression of revolted contempt. 'That bastard.' So! Pity or greed, neither were available to their frustrated employer. Yet he too was alone, could and would pay much more than the raddled old soldier down the corridor, with his rotting teeth and incontinent bladder. Barbara shook her head. The mysteries of sex! As hidden from her as from everyone else, except more so. 'I'll talk to Mrs Bracy,' she said. 'But Hannah...'

'Yes.'

'Whatever you do, please be careful. For my sake. I need you here.'

'The pay's good,' said the girl mutinously. 'You'd get someone else, no problem.'

'You don't understand,' said Barbara. 'I need you here as a friend.' She stalked out of the Dispensary and hurried down the corridor to Mrs Bracy's room. The old woman was still asleep, her breath coming in loud rasps, shaking her heavy frame.

'Mrs Bracy!' She bent down and shook the old woman, gently at first and then harder. Her eyes opened, vague but watchful. 'Mrs Bracy!'

'I'm trying to sleep.'

'I've just heard what you've said to Nurse Grant.' A sly smile flickered round the woman's mouth.

'If you so much as mention what you said again, in any way, I will have you out of here in twenty minutes. Do you understand?' Mrs Bracy closed her eyes, still smiling. 'Do you UNDER- STAND?' There was no reaction, only the maddening smile. 'Very well.' said Barbara firmly. 'I shall have you transferred this afternoon. God knows who'll take you, but your nephew Terence can deal with that.'

'Oh, I understand,' said her patient, opening one eye. 'I understand very well indeed. Don't worry though. I shan't breathe a word. She's a pretty little thing, isn't she? *Very* desir- able.' And with that, she began to snore again.

Chapter 10

If the spirit of autumn was spreading its nostalgic tendrils of decay over the whole city and county of Hampton, nowhere that Sunday morning were these tendrils more in evidence than over the castle and estate of Lodsworth, eleven miles south-east of the city. There, among the flaming woods, a sombre tower stood gaunt and empty, turning its blackened windows, like sightless eyes, onto a jungle of towering rhododendrons and heavy yews. The massive portico, its pillars strangled by thick tentacles of ivy, gaped down the avenue towards the remnants of a Gothic gateway, all crumbled masonry now, with just one bent pinnacle pointing an accusing finger at the encroaching brambles.

Yet, just as the forest trees continued to stand, despite their dying, falling leaves, so, in a glade beyond the wreck, a haze of fragrant grey smoke still hung above the low line of stable buildings, with their tattered grey shutters and mossy cobblestones. The two large stone troughs had been planted with pink sedum and one of the doors had been recently painted green and had a large brass door-knocker affixed to its centre. Overhead, the large slate face of the stable clock was innocent of hands, and its numerals were so faded as to be illegible. From time to time, however, the bell in the flaking white cupola fixed above the gable sent a clear note echoing through the trees, a note of defiance and survival, a chime of order in a disorderly world.

A glint of dazzling blue, just a flash, momentarily brightened the grimy mirror of the stagnant moat. The kingfisher had no time to stay to watch the new arrivals, two car-loads of men in creased suits, their faces showing different variations of unease. As the last door slammed shut, an old man dressed in baggy corduroys and a faded checked shirt hobbled round from the back of the stables, stopped and stared curiously at the little group.

'May I be of help?' He had an unkempt white beard but his voice, though soft, held authority.

'Yes,' said the leader of the group. 'We're looking for Lord Lodden.'

'And if you found him?'

'We're from British Rail. I've tried to telephone him, but there's no reply.'

'How did you get the number?'

The railwayman stared. 'From British Telecom.'

The old man grunted. 'It's supposed to be ex-directory,' he said. 'I'm Henry Lodden. What can I do for you?'

'Oh.' It was obvious they'd taken him for a

retired labourer. 'Well I'm the Deputy Area Supervisor for Hampton, and this,' he pointed to the shock-haired figure of Mr Bull, 'is my assistant.'

'Pleased to meet you.' The shabby master of the forest shook hands cordially with all of them. 'You're not planning a new line through here, I hope?' He appeared to have not one tooth in his head.

'No, indeed.' They all laughed dutifully. After a pause, the Supervisor said hesitantly, 'It's about your old branch line.'

'My what?'

'The line built by the old Railway Board to bring coal to the castle,' explained Bull.

'Good heavens!' The old man passed one hesitant hand through his straggling locks. 'That's been closed for years. I do just remember that it was still in use in 1937. That's when we had the fire, you know. I don't think it's been used since. Unless…'

'Unless?'

'Well,' the old man put his head on one side, 'unless the firm who cleared up used it for carting away some of the rubble. I've got a photograph of it somewhere, I think.' He had long white hairs growing out of his ears.

'We'd like to walk the line,' said the Supervisor, 'with your permission. There was some trouble last night on the main line.'

'I thought it still belonged to you.'

'No,' the men exchanged puzzled glances, 'the Estate bought it back under the original lease.'

'Oh yes!' The old man suddenly laughed. 'I do remember. We had some trouble over maintaining one of the bridges. It's a pity my nephew isn't here. He deals with all this nowadays. But you're very welcome to walk the line if you can find it.' He turned away, then added, 'But watch out for the trip-wires, will you? There'll be an awful to-do if you set off one of those damned things.'

Gingerly, the seven men made their way through the overgrown plateau that must once have been an elaborate rose garden, and down some mossy steps to the back of the ruin. There, amid heaps of fallen stone, they stared into the gaping cellars and wandered aimlessly about, wondering at so complete a wreck.

'Here it is!' A portly surveyor had followed one of the several pathways leading into the forest, and there, at his feet, was the rusted relic of a railway track. The others clustered round.

'Nothing's used that in living memory,' said Bull in disgust. 'This is a complete wild goose-chase!'

'The driver swore he saw an engine coming in from here,' said the Supervisor. 'Why else would he have braked so suddenly?'

'Hallucinations,' muttered Bull, 'or drink.'

'Come on,' was the reply. 'Now we're here, we'd better do the job properly.' Following the contour, they trudged over the golden leaves and through the clinging bracken. Overhead, the trees had long since met, forming a russet tunnel through which the old tracks, sometimes buried under generations of rotted compost, sometimes showing clearly through a patch of hard open ground, curved westwards towards the main London line. Gnarled tree-roots competed for space, grappling the metal with determined strength. Here and there the embedded sleepers had so rotted away that the track momentarily appeared to have sunk under the cindered soil. Once, only, the surrounding woods drew back and the ground suddenly plunged away on either side, as the line, now gleaming in the sun, was borne triumphantly across a deep ravine on a tall brick viaduct. On they went, led by the surveyor, their shoes increasingly stained by the dirt and their trousers matted with clinging burrs.

'A wild goose-chase.'

'Watch out!' The surveyor had glimpsed a sinister glint, the merest shimmer of reflected light from a thin wire drawn taut across their path.

'What is it?'

'Look! There!' Fascinated, they had followed the glittering wire into a thicket. Staked firmly into the ground, a small canister, shaped like a metal firework, presented a hostile mouth to the sky.

'A poacher trap,' said the surveyor, kneeling

down cautiously beside the sinister contraption. 'Touch the wire and it would go off like a bomb.'

'Would it kill?' The Supervisor could hardly believe it.

'No,' laughed the other. 'But it would alert the keepers. And give you a nasty fright. Come on, we must be nearly there.'

But it took nearly another hour of tramping through a series of overgrown cuttings before the shriek of a passing express alerted them to the approach of the main line junction. And there it all was, the ten trucks on their sides, skewed halfway over the churned-up embankment where last night's goods train had jumped the squealing points in its frantic effort to avoid the collision that its driver insisted had been imminent. Bill Evans, his cap pulled well forward over his ruddy face, was standing talking to his colleague as they watched the mobile crane at work. Seeing the sudden appearance of the men from the woods, he pulled off his cap and walked across the tracks to join them.

'You've got one line clear then?'

Bill nodded. 'The 10.46 has just gone through. I told you how it was,' he added smugly, pointing back into the trees, and trying not to laugh at the manager's bedraggled state.

'Rubbish!' The Supervisor was in no mood for humble pie. 'There hasn't been a train down there in your lifetime. Isn't that right?' he appealed to the others. They nodded.

'What about the greased points, then?'

'What points?' And indeed the nearside track for fifty yards in both directions was just a mangled fretwork of scrap metal.

'And Reg?'

'Dreaming.'

The old linesman turned away in disgust. 'There's none so deaf as them as won't be told,' he was saying, but he was saying it to himself.

Chapter 11

It was as Proby and Rootham were preparing to leave for Lincolnshire on Monday morning that Mr Rankin dropped by with the news that there would be an inquest on the dead robbers on Wednesday, and that they would be required to attend an informal inquiry by some official from the Director of Public Prosecution's Office immediately afterwards. 'No one doubts you, Jim,' he said, seeing the other's face fall. 'But they've got to go through the motions.'

'Am I to be suspended?'

'You've asked that before,' said Rankin. 'And the answer's no different: not while I'm in post.' He raised a hand in vague farewell and hurried down the corridor.

Fletcher and Houston was a company that believed less in advertising its presence than in discouraging visitors. There was no sign at the heavy gates on the side road leading into the little market town of Bagnaby, only a blind wall topped with broken glass, and a tinted glass guardhouse, from which, after repeated ringing, a man in a black tracksuit reluctantly emerged.

'Yes?'

Proby showed him his warrant-card. 'We've

got an appointment with Mr Simon Blencowe.'

The man examined the card carefully, and then stared at Rootham, before writing down their car registration number and disappearing into the guardhouse. After a long delay, during which Proby returned to the car and smoked a soothing cigarette, the great gates began to open, propelled by some unseen force. Twenty yards beyond them, a massive steel barrier had risen from the ground, and, as they approached it, three more guards, two of them armed, surrounded the car.

'Open the boot, please.'

'And the bonnet.' Proby did as he was told. It was all rather reassuring. And yet, less than a week ago, he and Rootham had both been at the wrong end of this company's products.

'All clear. You can go through now. You'll see my colleague beyond the second block.' The metal barrier silently sank back into the roadway. They drove past two warehouses and then across a large yard towards a uniformed guard who was waving them into a space between two large cars.

'Mr Blencowe is expecting you.' He gave them a rather half-hearted salute.

Blencowe, the managing director, was a tall man, thin to the point of emaciation, with receding red hair over a mottled cleanshaven face. He was wearing a neat pin-striped suit and a Brigade of Guards tie. He did not look pleased to see them.

'How may I help?'

Proby passed a large brown envelope across the empty desk. After an infinitesimal pause, Blencowe opened it and took out the ten by twelve inch glossy print. He stared at it without speaking.

'Is that one of yours?'

'It's got our name on it.' Rootham took out a notebook and began to write, ignoring the tall man's angry glare.

'I believe that it is the second to be recovered in the course of a crime during the last month?' Blencowe placed his hands together, forming a delicate Gothic arch with his fingertips. He said nothing. 'Is it possible that you could have had a break-in here?' Blencowe stared at his fingers. 'If we had,' he said at last, 'we would have reported it to our local police, and to the Home Office.' Rootham's pencil squeaked across the page.

'May we see your delivery records over the past, say, two years?'

Blencowe smiled. 'Certainly,' he said, 'if you can get a Home Office order and are personally covered by the Official Secrets Act.'

'Ted?' Rootham stopped writing, and pulled out another envelope from his briefcase.

Blencowe raised his eyebrows. 'I should have been warned about this,' he said angrily. 'I was simply told you wanted an interview, which I agreed to only out of courtesy to our local police.'

'We're very grateful,' said Proby smoothly. 'It saves a lot of time and trouble when everyone co-operates.'

'Trouble?'

'Well, only if you want to keep your licence.' A long silence followed.

'I'll have to consult about this.'

'Please do. Then I want the records.'

'Inspector...'

'Mr Blencowe?'

The tall man sighed. 'Very well.' He stood up, towering over them, and walked slowly out of the room. They could hear raised voices outside, then a door slamming.

'A real charmer.'

Proby grinned in agreement.

Blencowe came back in, still scowling, this time with another shorter man, similarly dressed.

'Hello, gentlemen! I'm George Lubbock. Let's see what we can do to help.' He shook hands with both policemen.

'And you are...?' Proby's face was bland, but firm.

'Me? Oh, I'm the general dogsbody.'

'And you're going to show us your delivery records?'

Lubbock bowed. 'I certainly am. Simon? Be a good fellow and fetch the offending documents, will you?' To Proby's immense surprise, Blencowe hurried to obey, returning almost immediately with a large ledger.

'Now.' Lubbock took the ledger and opened it. 'It's the 9 mm FH47s you're interested in, I'm told.' He looked up cheerfully and caught Proby's intrigued gaze. He winked. 'Here we are. Last year we manufactured exactly three thousand and delivered four thousand seven hundred and thirty, leaving just seventeen in stock. So far this year we have manufactured another two thousand and ten, and delivered only fourteen hundred. Take a look.'

'Leaving six hundred and twenty-seven in stock.' murmured Rootham, writing busily.

'Very quick!' said Lubbock admiringly.

'How often do you check your stock?'

'Every day.' It was Blencowe who answered.

'Could you have mislaid a couple?'

'Not if we wanted to stay in business,' Lubbock chuckled. 'No employee leaves the premises without an electronic check. Both of you, I'm afraid...'

'Of course.' Proby matched his smile. 'May we see where they're stored?'

Blencowe opened his mouth, but Lubbock interposed. 'But of course. Let's go together. Simon, will you do the honours?'

They all left the office, and walked across another yard to a low concrete building with a metal door set back between darkened glass windows.

'Armoured?'

'Of course.' Lubbock took out a small

plastic card and inserted it in a slot in the door, and then placed his fingers on a protruding metal plate. 'You see. State-of-the-art.' Very slowly the door swung open. There were two more electronic barriers to pass before they found themselves facing two long corridors, fined with weapons of all sizes. It was an impressive testament to Man's urge to kill. Two men in white coats were evidently engaged in a prolonged stocktake. 'Here we are. These are the 47s.'

They were stacked in boxes of twenty, each weapon carefully wrapped in greased cloth.

'What about substituting dummies?' Blencowe looked as if he might explode.

Lubbock shook his head and smiled. 'Nice idea, Inspector, but not possible. You can't really see, but every box sits on a computerized plate. A different weight, just a single milligram, would trigger an alarm.'

'And if you have a box of, say, only fifteen?'

'The computer is re-programmed. You would need a conspiracy involving half our staff to get a single gun out of here.'

'Is that possible?'

Lubbock put his head on one side and thought. 'It's possible,' he conceded, 'but it's highly unlikely. There are plenty of these in the outside world. It would be much cheaper to buy them from a military unit. You have to remember there are some fairly relaxed members at the eastern end of NATO.'

'But you don't supply those, do you?'

'No,' said Lubbock with a grin. 'But I bet you our products get passed around, even so.'

'That's your explanation?' Proby was becoming tired of the man's relentless bonhomie.

'Uh-huh. One thing I can tell you, they didn't come from here. If you let us have them back, I can tell you which batch they went in. All our products are numbered.'

'These weren't.' put in Rootham. 'The numbers were filed, right down.'

'How very inconvenient.' Lubbock shook his head. 'I think we'll have to keep rifling records from now on. What do you think, Simon?' Blencowe shrugged. He was sick of the whole thing, and wanted to get back to his routine. 'Anything else I can do for you gentlemen?'

Proby glanced at Rootham before shaking his head. 'Thank you both very much,' he said. 'It's been very illuminating.'

Chapter 12

'Are you sure you won't have dinner with me?'

Barbara shook her head with a smile. It was the third time Terence Bracy, Mrs Bracy's personable nephew, had dropped into her office to solicit a date.

'Or even lunch?' His blue eyes held a light and friendly plea. 'In a very public place of your own choice.'

'No, thank you. But it's nice of you to ask.'

'Oh, well.' He turned away to hide his disappointment. 'How is Aunt Betty?'

'Much the same as usual.'

He laughed. 'Meaning a real pain?'

She smiled back. 'It's difficult for her. We all understand that. It's why we choose to do these jobs.'

'Quite so.' He leaned over her desk. 'I'll go and pay my respects. Incidentally, I noticed the Dispensary door was open. Shouldn't it be locked?'

'Yes,' she said, rising quickly. 'It should. I'll go and see to it now.'

'Goodbye.'

'Goodbye.' She watched him walk away down the corridor before hurrying over to lock the Dispensary door.

It was nearly dusk, and the trees across the narrow lawn were beginning to lose their definition, retreating into the shadows and assuming their night-time roles as strange spiky presences, looming through the mist which curled up from the estuary beyond.

'It's beautiful.'

Barbara turned sharply to find Hannah standing beside her, staring out through the window. 'Yes,' she replied softly. 'This is so much my favourite time of year.'

'Season of mists and mellow fruitfulness?'

'Sorry?'

Hannah giggled. 'Come on,' she said, taking Barbara's hand. 'I've got a present for you. For being so nice to me.'

Between Dr Gresham's office and Barbara's was a small room originally intended for a typist. But one corner contained the boxed-in junction of all the heating pipes, and a fault in the insulation kept the room so uncomfortably hot that it had long since been abandoned by the perspiring typist and colonized as a store for equipment and half a dozen surplus armchairs.

'In here.' Hannah almost pulled Barbara through the door in her eagerness. 'Look!'

Balanced on the seat of an over-stuffed chair was a broad glass bowl filled with silk flowers. Ripe pink roses fought with glossy white lilies for space, amid a tangle of green fronds and speckled gypsophila. The whole array teemed with vigorous life and brilliant colour.

Barbara stared at her, unable to speak.

'Well?' Hannah's eyes were sparkling. 'Do you like them?' Barbara nodded. 'Give me a kiss, then!' Hannah opened her arms and Barbara meekly pulled the little nurse towards her, luxuriating in the warmth of the embrace. Abruptly she moved away. 'Thank you,' she said thickly. 'They're very nice.'

'You like me, don't you?' The little nurse had closed the door and was now watching the taller woman with a raw look of calculation. Barbara preserved her expression of detached calm, and then ruined the impression by swallowing noisily. 'I don't mind,' said Hannah, softly. Suddenly excited, she moved closer. 'Honestly I don't. Here.' She guided Barbara's trembling hand to the top button of her blue blouse. 'Come on,' she said, and laid her own hand against Barbara's stomach. 'Come on. See?'

Very slowly, their eyes fixed on each other, the two women unbuttoned their blouses. 'Let me.' Barbara undid Hannah's skimpy white bra and began to stroke her breasts. 'Oh God,' she sighed. 'Oh God!'

'Hang on!' Hannah turned briskly away, and with a deft wriggle, she was out of her skirt and tights, standing there, smooth and softly shadowed in the dim light from the corridor window.

'Is it really safe?' Barbara could hardly breathe, yet she could feel her heart thumping painfully. Clumsily, she undid her own skirt.

'Come here.' It was strange how nakedness had brought about a complete reversal of roles. Now it was the younger nurse, darting her tongue out like a sharp little adder, who commanded, and her heavier, taller companion who tenderly, even tremulously, obeyed, moving forward until their bodies just touched, sinking down, gasping with the spasms of desire that shook her belly. Behind the partition wall, his eye-socket pressed so hard against the peephole that the bone was beginning to ache, Dr Gresham watched them with astonished and agitated delight. And when, much later, Hannah let out a loud croaking cry, it was echoed by the doctor's own exhausted sigh. 'By God!' he muttered eventually, after wiping his mouth, 'that's for me. That is for me!'

Chapter 13

The following morning, the inquest on James Creasey, following immediately after that of Darren Gilbert, was opened shortly before eleven o'clock in the draughty Coroner's Courtroom in the County Council offices off Rufford Street. Rufus Blake, senior partner in a local firm of solicitors, had been Coroner for nearly twenty years, and was unused to the degree of press interest aroused by these deaths. Usually he experienced nothing more intrusive than George Pratt, the rangy ferret-faced reporter from the Hampton Gazette, sucking in his breath or breaking his pencil while scribbling down the sad little details of the city's occasional suicides.

Today, however, he had struggled past no less than three television crews and the brown-and-magnolia courtroom was packed with earnest types in anoraks, who stared at him with nothing like the respect he was accustomed to. While the Coroner's role in augmenting Crown income had passed into history, apart from the occasional case of treasure-trove (when some likely lad with a metal detector dug up another cache of Roman silver), his, and his jury's, role in determining the cause of death *super visum corporis* continued to earn him a useful addition to his annual income.

Normally he didn't even bother with a jury, but with murder as the inevitable verdict in the coming inquests on Hickock and the other victims, he had summoned, and sworn the jurors in for the whole day, just in case.

'Is the old bod with the barnet ever going to start?' mumbled a journalist.

'Silence please.' Blake opened his folder. 'This Court will come to order.' Surreptitiously, in the full gaze of three hundred eyes, he checked to see if his neat brown wig was safely and discreetly in position. It took years off him, whatever his wife said to the contrary.

The first witness was Major Sitwell, who gave evidence of identification, but before he was called, a stout man in his fifties, with greasy grey hair and heavy cheeks, stood up to identify himself as a Mr Gregory, a barrister who was acting jointly for the families of the dead robbers and for the 'Citizens for Safety'.

'Who?' The Coroner was mystified.

'The Citizens for Safety,' repeated Mr Gregory with a warm smile. 'A very public-spirited body.'

'No doubt,' sniffed Blake, 'but the jury and I would like to know what their exact interest in this inquest is?'

Mr Gregory bowed very low. 'I quite understand, sir. The Citizens for Safety are a group who take an interest in potential breaches of the law by law enforcement officers.'

'You mean, if you or I walked off with the Council silver? That sort of thing?'

'Not quite, sir.' Mr Gregory fixed the Coroner with a frosty look, not quite liking his flippant tone. 'In this case, they have an obvious...'

'One moment,' snapped Blake. 'I think we shall proceed faster if I acknowledge your right to be heard on behalf of the Creasey and Gilbert families. As for your other employers,' the Coroner's voice turned cooler, 'I think we may leave them to one side, don't you?' Mr Gregory shrugged, and risked a quizzical glance at the ranks of eager newspaper reporters. There was the gratifying sound of many pens scribbling on much paper.

After Major Sitwell had sworn to his identification of the two men, and answered all Rufus Blake's questions. Mr Gregory rose again.

'Major Frank Sitwell?'

'Sir?'

'These men served under your command?'

'Yes, sir.'

'In Northern Ireland?'

'Yes, sir.'

'In Kuwait?'

'Yes, sir.'

'In the former territory of Yugoslavia?'

'Yes, sir.'

'Mr Gregory?' The coroner leaned forward, his heavy eyebrows knitted together into a fero-

cious bar of bristling brown hairs, suggesting
what his head had once boasted before the need
for artificial camouflage.

'Yes, Mr Coroner?'

'This is only an inquest, you know.'

'*Only* an inquest?' Mr Gregory's eyebrows,
by contrast, rose individually into twin circum-
flexes above his rheumy eyes. 'That is not how my
clients see it. No, indeed. They see it as their one
chance to find out how their loved ones died.
How two fine young men, who fought long and
hard for their country, came to meet their lonely
deaths here in Hampton.'

'Not exactly *lonely*,' commented the Coroner
drily, 'since I shall be conducting four further
inquests on their victims this afternoon.'

'Alleged victims,' said Mr Gregory loudly.
'Alleged victims.' There was a long silence,
broken only by an old man coughing at the back
of the room. 'Now, if I may continue?'

Blake shrugged. 'Try not to take too long,
please.'

'Major Sitwell. Are you surprised that these
two fellow soldiers are alleged to have been
involved in armed theft and murder?'

The Major drew himself up and stared
directly at the Coroner. 'Very surprised indeed.
In fact, if I may speak…?'

'Go on,' said the barrister affably.

'Jim Creasey saved my life in Dubrovnik, and
Darren Gilbert was as straight a man as I could

ever hope to have beside me.'

'Two good men?'

'Yes, sir.'

'I wonder...?' Mr Gregory had turned to face the Coroner.

'Yes?'

'I see Detective Inspector Proby is in the courtroom.'

'Indeed he is.' Blake smiled across to where Proby, flanked by Superintendent Rankin and the police authority press officer, was skimming through the night's reports from the Incident Room. There had been two more reported sightings of the missing driver, but neither had come to much.

'I wonder whether he might want to cross-examine this witness?' Proby looked up and stared hard at the barrister.

'Now why would he want to do that?' enquired Blake.

'Because,' said Gregory very slowly, as if explaining a simple toy to a peculiarly stupid child, 'if the jury' (here he turned and bowed towards the group of bemused people sitting in a group to the Coroner's left) 'should conclude that there were a case for Mr Proby to answer arising from Mr Creasey's death, the evidence of this court would only be admissible if Mr Proby had been given an opportunity to cross-examine the relevant witnesses.'

'I see.' Rufus Blake ran an anxious hand

round the back of his wig, and then scratched his ear. 'I see.' He found it hard to believe that any sane man would question Proby's conduct, a policeman whose meticulous work he had observed and respected for twenty-five years, ever since he had started work in the city as a trainee solicitor in his father's firm. 'Detective Inspector Proby?'

Trying to disregard the urgent whisperings of the public relations officer, a smooth-faced woman who smelt of chewing-gum, Proby rose and shook his head. 'I have nothing to ask Major Sitwell,' he said quietly, and sat down again.

The second witness was Dr Milligan, who had performed both post-mortems. In Gilbert's case, death had been caused by four bullet wounds, piercing the heart and lungs and resulting in instantaneous death. As for Creasey, the impact of his fall had caused massive fractures of the skull on top of such internal damage as again to give multiple causes for death. Blake, who had had to view the bodies as part of his duty as Coroner, closed his eyes at the memory.

'Detective Inspector James Proby.' At the sound of his name, called out by the usher, Proby rose again and crossed to the plain wooden chair which was standing in as a witness-box. Having taken the oath, he sat down, as instructed, and calmly explained the events of the afternoon, starting with the call to his car to send him and Rootham careering down Stockard Street, and

ending in James Creasey's fall. When he had
finished, there was a prolonged silence. Everyone
was waiting to see how Mr Gregory would
proceed.

'Mr Proby.'

'Mr Gregory.'

'I want to be entirely fair with you.'

'Yes, sir.' Was there the faintest flicker of
irony in Proby's cold grey eyes?

'You have stated you came upon the scene
outside the post office shortly after the first shoot-
ings?'

'Yes, sir.'

'So you cannot know yourself who shot the
postmistress, or the two workmen?'

'No, sir.'

'Why did you pursue Mr Gilbert and Mr
Creasey?'

'In the first place, because Police Constable
Rivers, who was already there tending a wounded
witness, pointed me in the direction in which the
thieves had gone.'

'Whoever they might be?'

Proby nodded. 'Whoever they might be.
And in the second place, because when we drove
up Stockard Street, two men opened fire on us
before disappearing into the Gull Insurance
building.'

'Could you identify either man?'

'Only by their clothing. One man wore a red
anorak over black jeans, the other had on a green

military-style pullover and dark green slacks.'

'You were wounded in the hand, I believe?'

'Yes, sir.'

'But you had the time to get a very clear view of their individual garments?'

'Yes, sir.'

'Did you ever see either of these men again?'

'Yes, sir.'

'Oh, really?' Mr Gregory's voice rose an octave in assumed astonishment. 'And when was that?'

'On entering the building…'

'How much later?'

'Eight, ten minutes? Detective Sergeant Rootham and I had first taken up positions in Aubourn House, the block across the street, to keep the Gull building under surveillance.'

'So these fugitives might well have escaped out the back while you were doing this?'

'No, sir. They continued to fire at us from across the street.'

Mr Gregory sighed. 'Well, just remind me of your version then. You climbed the emergency stairs of the Gull building and found Mr Gilbert lying dead on the eleventh floor.'

'Yes, sir. He had his shotgun beside him.'

'*His* shotgun?'

Proby nodded. 'It only had his fingerprints on it, and the forensic test proved that he had recently fired it.'

Mr Gregory shrugged his shoulders. In truth, there was little enough here for him. The real purpose of his journey from London came next. 'You climbed on up to the roof?'

'Yes, sir.'

'Where you heard Mr Creasey calling for help?'

'Yes, sir.'

'Did you believe him to have shot Detective Sergeant Hickock?'

Proby paused to think. 'Yes, sir,' he said. 'His weapon was lying discarded on the roof. He was dressed as I described earlier. I did believe him to be the second fugitive.'

'Was that why you dropped him?' There was an immediate and total hush in the room. It had been quiet before, the odd whisper, the scratching of pencils, the occasional muffled cough. But suddenly people could hear themselves breathing, so dense and absolute was the silence in the courtroom. Even the air, warmed by grilles set in the stained oak floor, hung heavy, with floating particles of dust glinting in the autumn sunshine.

'One moment, Mr Gregory.' It was the Coroner again, and a very dirty look he gained from the barrister for his trouble.

'What is it, Mr Coroner?'

'You are putting a question to Inspector Proby the answer to which could possibly incriminate him.'

'I'm sure he is well aware of that, sir,' said the barrister angrily.

'Nevertheless,' went on Blake doggedly, 'under the Coroner's 1953 Rules, I am obliged to remind him that he need not answer such a question.'

'I'm sure he's properly grateful for your concern,' muttered Mr Gregory. 'Now, Inspector,' he said turning dramatically back to the policeman, 'don't answer me if you are afraid of incriminating yourself, but that is why you dropped him, isn't it?'

'No, sir.' Suddenly, shockingly, the sombre room was splashed with an explosion of lurid light, as a photographer in the second row stood up and snapped the confrontation between the two men, Proby leaning forward, his heavy face with its long sharp nose set in a mask of stolid truculence, Mr Gregory, in profile, lips and brow pushed forward, seeming to goad his prey into an admission of guilt.

'Mr Clerk! Bring that... that man here. Yes!' Blake was incoherent with indignation. The tiny clerk, bent and limping heavily, did his best to inject some sense of dignity into his halting progress across the room. The photographer, a good six foot six inches tall, his face half-hidden under long greasy black hair, towered over him, but meekly followed and came to a halt before the quivering Coroner.

'Your name, young man? Well?'

'Wensley Groves, sir.'

'And who do you represent?'

'I'm freelance, sir.'

'Don't you know that photography is strictly prohibited within this courtroom?'

'No, sir. I didn't.' His colleagues exchanged a few satirical looks.

'Hand over your film to the clerk.'

The tall man opened his camera, without protest, and handed over the contents, secure in the knowledge that the offending film was already in his neighbour's pocket. 'I should like to say that I'm very sorry, Mr Coroner.'

Blake sniffed. 'Quite so. As a Judge in a Court of Record, it is in my power to commit you for contempt arising within this courtroom. However,' he stared at the ranks of giggling journalists, 'we'll say no more about the matter on this occasion. The next man to follow your rash example will be taken straight to the cells.' The photographer walked slowly back to his place. 'Please carry on, Mr Gregory.'

'No? I asked you if that was why you dropped him, and you said *no*?' Mr Gregory's voice had risen to a squeak, and he cocked a sceptical eyebrow at the jurors, all dressed in quiet colours appropriate for their sombre duty. One man, older than the rest, had already shown signs of nodding off. Now he was alert again, his craggy face fixed on Proby's calm expression. 'Then why did you drop him? Tell us that.'

'I didn't drop him,' replied Proby flatly. 'He slipped out of my grasp.'

'How much do you weigh?'

'Fourteen and a half stone, sir.'

'Mr Creasey weighed just a hundred and fifty-four pounds,' said Mr Gregory, speaking with deliberate pathos. 'That's just about eleven stone. I'd have thought you could manage that, a strong man like you?' And indeed Proby did give off an air of enviable solidity, with his broad shoulders and chest.

'We were both sweating hard.'

'That doesn't sound like much of an excuse.'

'It was intended as an *explanation*,' snapped Proby, stung by the barrister's sneer. 'Not an excuse.'

Mr Gregory hid a smile. An angry witness is a malleable witness, likely to say more than he intends. 'You were angry, weren't you? Angry. about Sergeant Hickock.'

Proby narrowed his eyes, then shook his head. 'I was, later,' he said. 'But at the time, I was more frightened.'

'You! The scourge of Hampton's villains! A hardened thief-taker of fifty-six? Frightened? I find that rather hard to believe!' Mr Gregory winked at the jurors and was rewarded by a couple of unwary smiles.

'The gun involved fires sixteen rounds a second.'

'Yet by that time you knew he was unarmed, didn't you?' Proby nodded and remained silent. 'No, you decided not to wait for a trial. That was it, wasn't it? You wanted revenge. Vengeance is mine! For the loss of your colleague. Isn't that right, Inspector? Isn't that the truth of it?'

'Mr Gregory!' The Coroner had had enough.

'What now, Mr Coroner?'

'This is not a court of law, you know.'

'I do know that, sir. But *you* know that when you come to instruct the jury in determining the true cause of Mr Creasey's death, it is open to them to bring in a verdict of manslaughter, or indeed of murder.' An audible shiver ran round the room, a collective intake of breath that brought new expressions of extra concentration to the faces of the jurors. Murder! A police inspector! 'I'm sure you want them to be fully aware of the circumstances of Mr Creasey's death.'

Blake nodded reluctantly, and cast a despairing glance at his clerk. He had never been through anything like this before.

'No' said Proby, in a loud clear voice. 'I did not drop him. He slipped out of my grasp. It was an accident.' The oldest juror nodded his head in evident agreement.

'I don't believe,' said Mr Gregory insinuatingly, 'that you have ever expressed any regret?'

'Of course, I regret it.'

'Because you may face trial for murder.'

'Oh, no. Because Mr Creasey should have been tried for his crimes, and, if convicted, punished accordingly.'

'I see.' Mr Gregory paused and looked round at the room. 'Yet you speak of *his* crimes, as though you were certain of his guilt. Tell me, Inspector, do you believe in the death penalty?'

Proby shook his head. 'My private views are not relevant.'

'Oh, but I think they are,' smiled Mr Gregory. 'Pray share them with us.'

Proby stared at his tormentor. In fact, he was uncertain how to answer. His own experience led him to distrust the death penalty. Ever since an enterprising citizen named Daniel M'Naghten had taken a pistol to Sir Robert Peel, but killed his secretary by mistake, insanity had proved a convenient escape for those murderers whose crimes tended to support this 'defence'. Since these generally included child murderers, the very people whom he would be delighted to despatch personally, and since hanging terrorists tended to promote them as martyrs among their sympathizers, he saw little point in reserving death for the remainder, when genuine long-term imprisonment was as efficient in removing them from the community without any accompanying outcry.

'We're waiting.'

'On the whole,' said Proby, 'I'm against it.

It's a fine point, but yes, I'm against it. Just.'

'A *very* careful response,' sneered the barrister. 'So careful that I daresay it was carefully rehearsed.' The Coroner started to say something, but decided to stay silent. He was rewarded by Mr Gregory announcing that he had no further questions 'at this time' and Proby was allowed to return to his own seat, watched by the curious and speculative eyes of all present.

'There are,' said Blake in his direction to the jurors, having recapitulated the evidence presented, 'seven possible verdicts for you to consider in the case of Mr Creasey. I think we may discard natural causes or suicide' (a slight snigger from some of the press) 'and concentrate on accidental death, justifiable homicide, manslaughter or murder. If you cannot reach agreement, preferably a unanimous one but failing that with no more than two of you dissenting, on any of these, the seventh option is to return an open verdict, effectively saying that you find the evidence before you insufficient to reach a more explicit decision. 'This is entirely a matter for you: my only job from now on is to advise you as to the law involved.

'Accident means just what it says, an event over which no one had sufficient control to promote or to prevent. Justifiable homicide covers the deliberate or negligent causing of a death, whether in self-defence or, in the course of

upholding public order, where the person
responsible was acting properly, without dispro-
portionate violence, and without viable alternatives open to him. Manslaughter is where the
death arose from negligent conduct or through
provocation. Murder can only be chosen where
there are reasonable grounds to believe that the
person responsible either deliberately intended
to cause the death, or alternatively, acted in such
a way that death or serious injury could reason-
ably be expected as a possible outcome. To illus-
trate these alternatives to you in this case,
justifiable homicide was your verdict earlier this
morning in the case of Mr Gilbert, and this could
also apply to Mr Creasey if you believed that
Inspector Proby was seriously at risk himself if he
had not released his grip. Accidental death would
apply if you believe that Inspector Proby was
trying to save Mr Creasey, but the latter slipped
from his grasp. Manslaughter would apply if for
example Inspector Proby had negligently done
something to put Mr Creasey at risk on the roof.
As to murder,' he was making valiant efforts to
maintain an even-handed tone, 'this would mean
either that Inspector Proby deliberately dropped
Mr Creasey to his death, or that he was so negligent in his rescue attempt that he must reason-
ably have anticipated death as a likely result. If
you decide on a verdict of murder or manslaughter, it is open to you to name the person
you believe to be guilty, by way of a rider to your

verdict.' He sat back, exhausted, unaware that, in his agitation his wig had slipped sideways, causing considerable mirth among the ranks of the pressmen.

Five minutes later, the jury returned their second unanimous verdict of the morning: James Creasey, an unemployed male aged thirty-six of no fixed address, had died from multiple fractures of the skull at 18.24 hours on Friday the seventh of October 1994, having fallen from the roof of 63-67 Circle Road, Hampton, while attempting to evade arrest. The cause of his death was accidental.

'It was only to be expected,' remarked Mr Gregory grumpily to a thin man with a wispy red moustache who had sat beside him, while the inquisition form was being signed by the jurors before the court adjourned for lunch. 'Local people, and a hostile Coroner. No sense of the dramatic.'

'Don't worry,' replied the other, fingering his moustache with a smile. 'We shan't stop now. You'll have plenty of chances to be dramatic before we've finished with that sodding copper. Come on. Let's be moving. We've got ten minutes to catch the London train.'

Chapter 14

While the train carrying Mr Gregory and his foxy companion sped through the Lodsworth woods under the admiring gaze of the men working to repair Friday night's damage, Proby was being ushered into another office in the Council complex which had been made available for the Department of Public Prosecution's team.

'Come in, Inspector.' There were three of them, a thick-set woman with grey hair swept back into a bun, who rose as he came in, flanked by a younger man in a blue three-piece suit on her left, and another man, narrower and totally motionless, who sat up very straight on her right. 'This is Rupert Collins, my assistant, and Mr Smith, who keeps an eye on things for the Home Office. My name is Marion Darby.' The younger man acknowledged Proby's nod with a shy smile, but Mr Smith just stared at him, his face wholly without expression or movement. 'Do please sit down.'

'Thank you, Mrs Darby.'

'It's Miss, actually. Now, you do know you are entitled to legal representation if you want it?'

Proby nodded. He had been through all this with Rankin and with the Chief Constable, not to mention repeated calls from the Police Federation lawyers. To tell the truth, he wasn't much bothered. It all depended on whether they believed him or not. No amount of legal tricks was going to change that, and at his age, he had grown accustomed to standing on his own and he wasn't going to hide behind some retained London hack just to make the Federation feel they were being useful. 'I know that,' he said flatly.

'But you choose to waive that right?'

'Yes.' The younger man had switched on a tape-recorder, and was also taking notes in long-hand.

'We understand the inquest verdict was "accidental death"?'

'That's correct.'

'You must be very relieved.'

He raised his eyebrows. 'No,' he said. Mr Smith still hadn't budged at all, his stony stare seeming to bore into Proby's head. Perhaps this was standard Home Office intimidation.

'There is a suggestion that a private prosecution may be brought against you.'

'So I've heard.'

'Rupert, turn off the tape for a moment.' The young man obeyed. 'Now, Inspector, I want to go off the record for a moment.' She smiled winningly, and he smiled back, well aware that a second, concealed, recorder would be beavering away. 'All of us can readily sympathize with your actions. I'd have dropped the bugger myself...'

She paused. He said nothing. 'But we do need to know, for our own purposes, exactly what happened...'

'There's no secret about it,' he said flatly. 'I tried to pull him up. He wasn't particularly heavy. He just slipped away. That's all there was to it.'

'Rather convenient, wasn't it?' Mr Smith's mouth hardly seemed to move.

Proby shrugged. 'Not for me. Look at all this hassle. I should be out there finding the driver, not tied up in here.'

'We have to do our duty,' murmured the young man.

'Oh, yes,' smiled Proby. 'I'm not complaining. I'm just making the point that there was nothing in it for me.'

'No one would blame you for giving way to anger. Mr Hickock was a good friend.'

'Not particularly. But either way, my job is to take villains, not kill them.'

'Quite.' She leaned back with a sigh. 'I'm only trying to make it easy for you.' Her smile was very insincere.

Proby matched it. 'And I'm very grateful,' he said. 'It's just that I didn't drop him.'

'Switch that thing back on again!' She was beginning to flag. 'Now take us through the whole scene again, step by step.'

An hour later, they were no further, and, with very poor grace, she told Proby he could leave.

When he reached home, Proby found a smart little red sports car parked outside his house.

'Jim! This is Raquel, from the Social Services.' Sheila had a tense air, her voice was husky, and she looked as if she'd been crying.

'Hello, Jim.' Raquel was a short pretty woman of about thirty, with black hair cut very short and vivid red lipstick. She stuck out her hand, which he shook, reluctantly, and then took himself off to the windowseat, momentarily distracted by the flocks of small birds swirling together round the telephone poles. It was time for their great migration, their odyssey to unknown southern lands, whence they might never return.

'Sheila tells me you're a policeman?'

'Yes.'

'You're a Detective Inspector?'

'That's right.' He glared at her, daring her to make some facetious comment. He had had enough interrogations for one day.

'And your annual salary?'

'Is this strictly necessary?'

'Jim, *please*.'

'£26,946 plus a £500 detective allowance.'

'I see.' She pursed her lips. 'Any overtime?'

'When he can be bothered to claim it,' put in Sheila in an exasperated tone.

'How much last year?'

'About fifteen hundred.'

'His sergeant takes home more than he does.'

'How much is your mortgage here?'

'Raquel.'

'Yes, Jim.'

'Just how is that any of your business?'

'Sheila's told me she rarely earns more than about five thousand pounds doing her shop-work. I need to assess your joint budgets to see if you can afford to bring up a child without threatening your lifestyle.'

'Why?'

'Because some adults get very rigid in their habits. And if the child threatens their expenditure on themselves, that can lead to an unloving environment.'

'Our mortgage is with the Halifax. It costs us a hundred and eighty pounds a month and has about four years to run.'

'It's interest and repayment?'

'Yes, thank goodness.'

'I see.' She gave a thin smile. 'What are your prospects of promotion.'

'None.'

'Oh? Why's that?'

'Because,' said Sheila heavily, 'he doesn't want it. Do you?'

'No.' he admitted. 'I don't. I like my work. And I don't like my desk.'

Raquel raised her eyebrows and made some notes. 'You both seem rather old to be adopting…'

'I'm only thirty-nine,' put in Sheila eagerly.

'And John's a very active fifty-six. We'd give a little baby all our love.'

'Hmmm. We do normally have an upper limit of forty for Mum and forty-five for Dad.' Raquel was re-reading her notes, and not liking what she saw. 'Which of you can't have children?'

'Mind your own bloody business!' snapped Proby, his face red with indignation.

Sheila leapt out of her chair. 'Jim! Just answer her questions. She's here to help. Why are you being so *fucking* aggressive?' Raquel's face was a picture.

He sighed. 'You've probably forgotten,' he said, 'but I've spent the whole day being cross-questioned by people trying to make me admit to murder.' He tried to smile, and failed.

'I had forgotten. Jim's had a dreadful time, lately,' she added for Raquel's benefit.

'Don't tell me you're the man who let that soldier drop?'

Proby threw himself into his chair. 'Yes,' he growled. 'That's me. Hampton's walking talking mass-murderer. The copper who can't pinch a shoplifter without blowing her away.'

'Oh darling,' Sheila came and knelt beside him. 'It's not like you to let them get at you.' She took his hand and squeezed it.

Raquel closed her notebook with a snap. 'I'm sorry,' she said, standing up. 'I'll see myself out. Thanks for the tea.'

'You're not going?'

'I must.' Her eyes held a pinched look, and her mouth was set in a rictus of distaste. 'You'll get notification in due course.'

'But there must be more questions you need to ask?' Sheila was standing, pleading.

'Not really.' She turned neatly away and walked to the door. 'Goodnight.' The door shut firmly behind her.

Sheila stared at her husband. 'I don't think she liked you,' she said after a pause.

'I'm sorry, love.'

'Look out.' She dumped herself heavily on his lap and threw her arms round his neck. 'Now listen.' He looked up into her burning eyes. 'I love you very much,' she said. 'I know I haven't been a perfect wife. And I would love us to have a little baby.'

He nodded sadly. 'I know.'

'I do love you. And I'd rather have you as you are, than a child with anyone else.' She loosened his tie. 'Shall I get you a drink? Then you can tell me about the Spanish Inquisition.'

Chapter 15

'How's your leg?'

'Worse' The man's beard was matted with sweat, and his breathing was coming in short, wheezing gasps.

'Let me see.'

'NO!' He cried out at the thought of the pain that would follow. Half his body was throbbing now, and he could feel his heart pulsing the blood through his distended chest. 'I need a doctor.'

'It's too dangerous. There's no one we can trust.'

'Then for pity's sake turn me in. I'd rather be in Parkhurst than this filthy hole.'

'You should have thought of that before coming here. We had a perfectly good arrangement to cover anyone getting caught.'

'I'm sorry.' The man seemed completely exhausted. 'I just wanted to get away. They'd have killed me too.'

'Nonsense! The British policeman doesn't shoot an unarmed fugitive.'

'That bastard dropped Jamie.. didn't he?'

'Perhaps.'

'There you are then. Oh GOD!' He groaned again, and started to whimper.

'I've brought you some more rum.' There was no reply. 'And the Sun.'

'I need a fucking doctor.' It was just a whisper, barely audible.

'I'll see what I can do. You're perfectly safe here.'

'Safe for you, you mean.'

'It's the same thing.'

'What if I die?'

'I'll bury you myself. Now cheer up, the fever will pass, and then we'll get you out of here.'

'I want to see a doctor.'

'I know. I've said I'll see what I can do.'

'Dr Gresham!'

'Yes, Barbara?'

'It's Mrs Bracy. She's dead.'

'Damn!' He put down his morning paper and stood up. 'What did you do? *Beat* her to death?'

'No.' She shook her head seriously. 'She died in her sleep. Hannah found her when she went to check her just now.'

He looked at his watch. 'But it's nearly nine forty-five.'

'We've been letting her sleep on. I looked in at about seven, and she seemed asleep. There really didn't seem any point in disturbing her.'

'I didn't realize you came in before eight?' he said, with an ironical glint in his eye that she didn't quite like.

'I slept over. I was worried about Mr van Oss again.'

'Oh, indeed? And how is Mr van Oss now?'

'He's fine.'

'Well, that's something. I suppose I'd better take a look at our corpse. Damn!' She followed him down the corridor, aware of searching glances from other members of the staff who were just beginning their day. A death in the building, however much it might be expected, always brought tension and uneasiness in its wake. There is a mystery, an awe, not about dying but about that final convulsion, the moment when all the questions of life and all the sorrows are resolved. Suddenly it is finished, and matters so very little that it is hard to recall why it ever seemed so excruciatingly vital. Even Mr Judd the louche Head Porter seemed subdued, hardly raising his massive head from the corner desk where he was sorting the day's post.

'I'd hardly have recognized her!' And indeed, in death, Mrs Bracy seemed to have shrunk in upon herself. With life, and its accompanying streak of malice, fled, the little old woman was greatly diminished. Dr Gresham shook his head. 'Eight hundred guineas a week!' A sad loss indeed.

'I've rung Mr Terence Bracy, her nephew.'

'Heartbroken, no doubt!'

'He sounded quite calm and businesslike. He's coming over at lunchtime.'

'Undertakers?'

'I recommended Brigg and Brogan, of course, and he said he'd probably use them.'

'Good. Don't forget to remind them about our commission. I'll need to sign the death certificate if you can find me the form.'

'No post-mortem?'

'Good God, no. Eternal rest has come right on cue for Mrs B, if not for our cash-flow. Deal with all the bureaucracy, will you, and then come and see me There's something else I want to talk to you about.' He winked.

'May I ask what it's about?' she said frostily.

'That little nurse of yours.'

She stared at him, praying to be armoured against a blush. 'Miss Norton or Mrs Harston?'

'Neither,' he said, with a wolfish grin. 'Hannah... um... Grant.' He turned away, chuckling to himself. He was going to have a good time from now on, that much was very certain. As he neared his office, he could hear the telephone ringing, and hurried to take it.

'Peter Gresham speaking.'

'I'm glad I've found you.' An authoritative voice.

'Hang on.' He put down the receiver, and went over to close the door. 'Sorry about that. We've lost a patient this morning, that's why I've been tied up. Rather a valuable one, as it happens.'

'Never mind that now. I need to see you.'

'Come here. I'll give you an excellent lunch and a good bottle of claret.' He tried to sound enthusiastic.

'No, it's too urgent for that.'

'Can't we do it over the telephone?'

'No. You'll have to come here.'

'Are you at home?'

'Yes.'

'It's not easy this morning.'

'Do I need to remind you how much you owe me?' The voice held an angry timbre.

'Of course not,' said Dr Gresham, suddenly breathless. 'But…'

'I'll expect you in forty minutes.'

There was a decisive click as his caller hung up, then a tap at the door, and Barbara, rather red in the face, peered in. 'You wanted to see me?'

'Later,' he snapped. 'I've got to go out.'

'But Mrs Bracy… the death certificate…'

'It'll just have to wait,' he snapped. 'She isn't going to run away, is she?'

'But…'

'Just deal with it yourself!' He was suddenly furious. 'What do I pay you and Dr Singh all this money for? Let him sign the damned thing, for Heaven's sake. It won't bite him. I'll talk to you when I get back.'

Only the image of her idyllic home kept her from throwing her clipboard at him. 'Very well,' she said, mastering herself. 'I'll look forward to it.'

'So shall I.' He pushed past her, and almost ran down the corridor.

Chapter 16

Back in the stench and clatter of the long low Incident Room off Jewgate, Proby was being given a detailed review by Mr Renfrew, the Office Manager, whose job it was to supervise the team of eight officers who dealt with receiving, indexing and researching the various reports on twelve-hour shifts.

'Nothing very solid,' grumbled Proby, after sifting through the papers for the third time, and absent-mindedly initialling the overtime sheet.

'Mrs Sentance wants to have a word.'

'I thought she was on night-duty.'

'She is, but she's stayed behind to see you. She's got a theory.'

'I'll see her in your office. It's too noisy in here. Give her a strong cup of coffee.'

'And you?'

'Thanks.'

'Fag?'

'Why not.' Proby took the cigarette and stuck it in his mouth. He had hardly slept the night before, kept awake by the light from the street lamp and by his troubled thoughts. Had he dropped Creasey on purpose? And if so, had he lied on oath? The whole of that frenetic evening had retreated into an opaque haze at the very back of his mind. He remembered reaching down. He remembered Creasey's triumphant smile as he began to haul him up. He remembered twisting his wrists. And he remembered, all too clearly, the man's horrified expression, as he rocketed away into the void. Clearest of all, he remembered Hickock's skull, laid shockingly bare and splintered by the force of the bullets.

'Sir?'

'Come in, Mrs Sentance. You must be worn out.' She stared at his ravaged face, the rumpled skin grey from lack of sleep, the sharp chin blurred by a patch of grey stubble. 'No,' she said with a smile. 'I feel very alert really.' She passed him his coffee.

'Now, let's hear what you've got.'

'Well.' She took off her spectacles and gave them a nervous polishing with a pink piece of tissue paper. 'I'm suggesting making two assumptions: one, that the driver was hit by shrapnel. After all, there was a lot of metal flying around, witness that poor old lady from Stockard St Peter Street Post Office. Two, that all the negative sightings are wishful thinking.'

'So?'

'So he's holed up somewhere in, or just outside, the city. He will certainly be needing urgent medical attention. After all, that old lady has lost a leg.'

'And?' He, was trying hard to concentrate.

'He's hardly likely to present himself at

Hampton General. So what if we kept a discreet surveillance on that list of iffy doctors?'

'Iffy doctors!'

'Yes. The drug squad have pinpointed six who regularly feature as over-prescribing Morphine and Valium.'

'We'd be in real trouble with the BMA if it got out!'

'So we do it very carefully.'

'Hmm.' He leaned back in his chair, and almost dropped straight off to sleep. He shook his head vigorously. 'Yes!' he said, to her surprise. 'It's an excellent idea. Who's on duty as Action Allocator?'

'Sergeant Haines.'

'Get it in place.'

'You look all in.'

'So do you.' He grinned. 'I'll live. Just get it done. And let me have the list so I can warn Mr Rankin.'

He had agreed to meet Sheila for lunch in a new café which had opened in Broad Street. Wearily, he pulled on his jacket and walked out into Jewgate, a narrow street made darker by its tall timbered buildings, with their over-hanging eaves, which leaned towards each other like gossiping neighbours. For five hundred years, this street had barely changed. No doubt it was cleaner now that the horses had given way, first to motorists, but now only to pedestrians. Looking along it now, thronged with hurrying shoppers, he reflected that whoever had tried to keep the peace in 1491, when Isaac Cope, commemorated by a smart stone plaque, had given two freeholds to the Parish Chest, would have recognized the same scene. He wouldn't have had to face trained soldiers wielding hand-held machine-guns – although, Proby reflected, a couple of Tudor ruffians whirling mace-and-chains above their heads might have been equally daunting at the time.

'What on earth are you grinning about?' Mollie Rootham, Ted's diminutive wife, had emerged from a shoe shop, and was staring at him. 'Ted said they gave you a right roasting.'

'No worse than expected,' he said.

'If it was up to me, we'd drop the whole lot over a precipice.' Seeing his frown, she added hastily. 'Nothing's going to get in the way of this Thursday?' The two couples made a practice of meeting each week for a good supper and a game of cards.

'Certainly not. It's our turn to win.'

'Are you meeting Sheila?'

He nodded. 'At this new place. Mario's, or something like it.'

'Tell me what it's like. I've got to rush. The twins are rehearsing for the school play. *My Fair Lady*, would you believe?' She hurried away, and he watched her trim figure's precise progress through the crowds. He'd have loved to have a daughter. But then, maybe Sheila filled that role too. There'd been plenty of times he'd been called upon to exercise parental restraint.

Mario's turned out to be a shallow corner-shop converted into a café bustling with ethnic Italian atmosphere and fittings, with an ice-cream counter and a massive copper expresso machine that frothed and hissed like a beached sea-monster. Dimly visible through the steam, a massive old woman with reams of black hair piled high upon her head shouted obscure orders to a tiny man in tight trousers who ran this way and that with seemingly inexhaustible bonhomie.

'*Si signor?*'

'I'm looking for my wife.'

'Wouldn't mine do?' The little man rolled his eyes and flapped his hand horizontally. '*Ah-yi-yi!* The signoras! But where would we be without them?'

Proby smiled politely. 'I'll wait here.' He sat down at a gaily clothed table and helped himself to an olive.

'MARIO!' The proprietor scuttled away.

'There you are.' Sheila, her pretty face glowing from the exertion of climbing up from the riverside carpark, sat down beside him.

'*O! Che bella bambina!*' Mario was back. 'You never said, signor. You never told me your wife was, mmm, *bellissima!*'

'No,' said Proby, shortly.

'A nice bottle of chianti? Bottled specially by my own brother?'

'We'd like to see the menu.' Proby turned on his best 'I-drop-people-off-tall-buildings' look, and the man slunk away, abashed.

'He's sweet,' said Sheila, pulling off her scarf and shaking out her long blonde hair to the great distraction of three young men at the neighbouring table.

'Up to a point.'

'Are you jealous?' She smiled up at him.

'A bit.'

'Mr and Mrs Proby! How nice to see you.' A young waitress, with red hair and freckled skin, had come over with a basket of bread.

'It's Wendy, isn't it? We wondered where you were working now,' said Sheila.

'Oh, I move about a bit.'

'I'm glad you haven't learnt Italian,' muttered Proby.

She laughed. 'Oh, Mario's okay. It's Mrs Mario who's a bit of a pain. What would you like?'

'Do you do spaghetti carbonara?'

'Of course.'

'Let's have two of those, two green salads and a bottle of sparkling mineral water.'

'Coming right up.'

'It's nice to see you, Wendy,' said Sheila.

'And you.' The girl hurried through to the back of the café and disappeared out of sight behind a bogus rubber plant.

'You look tired, Jim.'

'So everyone tells me.'

'You didn't sleep very well, did you?'

'You couldn't have done more to help.'

She giggled. 'You bruised me.'

He took her hand. 'I've got a few scars too. I want to talk some more about adoption.'

Her face darkened. 'No,' she said. 'It was a mistake. I know that now.'

'We could start again from scratch.'

'No.'

'I had another idea.'

'Oh yes?'

'What if you were able to conceive with… well, with… someone else?'

She stared at him. 'You can't be serious.'

'Well…' He dropped his eyes. 'I know this is important to you.'

'Not as important as our marriage, thank you.'

'But…'

'Don't say, it,' she hissed. 'Don't *bloody* say it!'

'*Signor*! *Signora*! *Pace, pace*. Only my wife speaks to me like that.' The wiry little proprietor had returned with two glasses of foaming red wine. 'See! A free glass for both of you. To toast my success with this fine establishment!' They glowered at him. 'Please. To Mario and Dorabella. *Sante*!'

Reluctantly they both drank. It was delicious. 'Thank you,' said Sheila. He looked at Proby.

'Thank you,' said Proby.

'And now I leave you in peace.' There was a prolonged silence.

'I know,' said Sheila carefully, 'that you haven't had much reason to value my fidelity.' He made a negative gesture with his hand. 'Don't interrupt me, please. It's true. But you have got to believe me that that is in the past. If we can't have children, that's sad, but it's not intolerable. You sending me out to be covered like a dairy cow is intolerable. Have you got that?' Her eyes were burning, and her cheeks were bright red. The three young men were watching her open-mouthed. Proby nodded. 'Now I never want to hear another word on the subject. Clear?'

'Very clear.' Proby squeezed her hand, grateful that his squad couldn't witness this scene.

'Two spaghetti carbonara and two green salads.' 'Thank you, Wendy.' They ate ravenously.

Chapter 17

'Are you all right?'

Barbara, looking in on Dr Gresham's office that afternoon, found him slumped over his desk. A half-empty bottle of vodka helped explain his heavy raucous breathing.

He looked up, his eyes bloodshot and his mouth sagging on one side. For a moment she thought he'd had a stroke. 'No,' he said. 'I'm not all right.'

'Anything I can do?'

'Yes.' he said, eyeing her figure through the haze. 'I'm going to fuck you senseless in a minute.'

'*What?*' She could hardly believe what she'd heard.

'You heard. If you can let yourself go with little Miss Hannah, you can certainly give me a piece of the action.'

'Dr Gresham!'

'Close the door and take your clothes off.' His speech was very slurred.

She walked over and slapped his face, very hard, twice. 'Don't you ever speak to me again like that.'

'Hoity-toity.' His eyes seemed to clear and he began to laugh softly. 'I saw you. Sucking that little tart inside out. That wouldn't look too good on a matron's CV, eh?'

She could feel her cheeks burning, and her heart pumping uncomfortably fast. 'I don't know what you mean.' 'It sounded pretty thin, even to her.

'"*There, oh there. Lower.*"' He was mimicking her. 'I heard you. What a performance, two pretty maids together. But I'm broad-minded. I shan't say anything.' Sweat was pouring off his brow, and twice he wiped it away on his trousers. 'But after what I've seen and done today, I've earned some relaxation.' He slumped down in his chair. 'Please be nice to me.'

'What have you seen today?' Anything to get him off the subject.

He shook his head dolefully. 'Dreadful. Dreadful.'

'Where?' She was becoming quite interested, despite her shock and disgust.

'Nowhere' He made an obvious effort to pull himself together. 'Forget what I said.'

'It's not going to be easy.' She felt damp and exhausted. You didn't get this sort of thing at Queen Charlotte's! He must have actually been watching them. Or tape-recording. A video? She swayed at the thought. How could they have been so stupid? As for sex with Dr Gresham! The mere thought made her want to retch.

'I'm sorry,' he said. 'I've had a shock.'

'So have I,' she snapped, and walked out, slamming the door. 'Hannah!'

'Yes, Matron?' By good luck, she had just come out of the store opposite.

'Can you come to my office, please?'

'Certainly, Matron.' Her dark eyes were full of mischief.

'It's serious.'

'Oh?'

Barbara ushered her into the office and closed the door. 'Gresham knows'

'*Gresham knows!*' Hannah covered her mouth with one hand. 'How?'

'I don't know. I don't like to think how. But he does. He's just propositioned me.'

'You sure he wasn't joking?'

'Hannah, *believe* me. He wasn't joking.'

'Kiss me.'

'Hannah ...'

'Just kiss me.' Barbara did as she was told. 'I like you.'

'And I like you.'

'So. I'll think of something to pay him back. Stuff old Gresham and his dreadful sagging pot belly!'

'That's just what I don't want to do!' But Barbara was calm now, and laughing. 'I can't tell you what he looked like. He kept mumbling about a shock he'd had.'

'Do we care? We're both adults and there's no law against a bit of slap and tickle.'

'I know.' Barbara sat down. 'Are you free tonight?'

'I certainly am. Indian or Chinese?'

'Come home with me. I'll cook you a memorable chilli con carne.'

'What makes you think you'll have time?' They were both still laughing when Dr Singh looked in to check the next day's surgery list.

'You ladies look cheerful.'

'We are, Doctor, we are.'

'That's lucky. Because I'm going to need all your help getting through this list tomorrow. Dr Gresham doesn't look at all well.'

Chapter 18

'They've done it. They've bloody gone ahead and done it!' Detective Chief Superintendent Rankin was staring at the fax with stupefied outrage.

'Done what?' Proby was too busy lighting a cigarette to pay much attention to the piece of paper Mr Rankin's secretary had hurried in with.

'They're bringing a private prosecution against you for murder. The sodding "Citizens for Freedom".'

Proby sat back in his chair. 'Christ!'

'You may need him, mate. Excuse me, I'm going straight up to see the Chief.' He lumbered out. Proby, left alone, stared at his nails. The telephone rang, and he picked it up.

'This is Mills, sir. We've just had an anonymous caller. She says there's been a murder at the Hampton Clinic. A Mrs Bracy.'

'Trace it?'

'Callbox just outside the Clinic. 17.53 hours. We recorded it of course. Shouldn't be difficult to identify the caller. It's obviously one of the staff. Do you want me to pass it through to DI White?'

'No thanks. I need something to take my mind off things. I'll go up there now. Find DS Rootham and tell him to meet me there.' He met Mr Rankin coming back down the corridor.

'Where are you off to?'

'Routine call at the Hampton Clinic. Disgruntled staff say there's been a murder. I'm just checking it out to give myself a bit of light relief.'

'Why not let White take it? Haven't you got enough to do? They'll be serving a summons first thing tomorrow. You're to appear at Trant Street Magistrates' Court at 10 o'clock. The Chief is raising Cain on your behalf which makes a nice change.'

Proby dredged up a smile. 'Well, I'd better get on with it, hadn't I? I don't want to appear in the papers as a fugitive from justice. By the way, we've just identified the driver. John Edward Holland. Lived with Creasey's sister in Pickerwick. They were all close mates in the army. I reckon the officer could have told me that straight off if he'd wanted to.'

'All you've got to do now is find him.'

'We'll find him.' Proby waited two minutes for the lift, and then ran impatiently down the stairs. He certainly wasn't going to neglect this new problem, imaginary or not.

'Sir!' It was the Desk Sergeant. 'I've got a bit more background on Mrs Bracy for you. She died this morning, and they've moved the body to Brigg and Brogan's mortuary chapel off Circle Road.'

'Who signed the death certificate?'

'A Dr Singh.'

'Is he the Medical Director?'

'Can't say, sir. That's all I've got so far.'

'Thanks anyway. I'll take a look at the body first. Tell Rootham, would you?' He hurried out into the twilight and it was only when he reached his car at the far end of the chain-fence that he realized he had left the keys in his office.

'This is Elizabeth Bracy.' Mr Brogan was a stocky man with warm eyes and a large pink double chin. 'Did you know her yourself?'

'No.' Proby stared down at the shrunken corpse dressed, unexpectedly, in a lilac woollen cardigan over a grey silk blouse. The lower half was hidden under a white wrap. 'Do you always dress your bodies like this?'

'Oh, no, sir.' Mr Brogan laughed very heartily. 'But we do exercise our imagination. It's surprising what you can find out about a person's taste by examining their body.'

'Quite.' Proby had no desire to enquire further. 'May I see the death certificate?'

'I have a copy here.'

'"Myocardial infarction." Tell me, who is Dr Singh?'

'A very nice gentleman. We know him well.'

'Do you get a lot of work from the Clinic?'

'Well, now.' Mr Brogan's face assumed an expression of deep professional caution. 'No health establishment would exactly say it lost a *lot* of patients, if you understand me.'

'But those who do inadvertently die in the Hampton Clinic are likely to come here?'

Mr Brogan bit a fingernail. 'Yes,' he said. 'That gives a fair approximation.'

'Because you pay a commission?'

'All perfectly legal, Inspector.'

'Of course. I'm just trying to get the background. Now, Dr Singh. He is the Head of the Clinic?'

'No, no. Dr Gresham is the Head. I'm sure you must know him. A very nice gentleman indeed.'

Proby shook his head. 'And the next of kin? Who will pay your fees?'

'Mr Terence Bracy. He was Mrs Bracy's nephew. He's next year's Chairman of the Chamber of Commerce, and he was City Sheriff two years ago. You'll know him.'

'I think I do remember the name,' said Proby grudgingly. 'Doesn't he run Kew and Bracy, the jewellers?'

'That's him. A very fine businessman.'

'Right. Let's see the body.'

'*See the body*?' Mr Brogan's voice sank to a whisper.

'Yes. Can you take all this stuff off. I need to do a thorough examination. I'm expecting Detective Sergeant Rootham and I'll start as soon as he arrives. We'll need to have a post-mortem arranged. Dr Milligan will contact you later tonight.'

'But why? Mrs Bracy's just a harmless old lady who died of a heart-attack in her sleep, while under medical care.'

'You know that. Dr Singh knows that. Maybe even I know that, but sometimes we have to carry out these procedures, just to keep everyone happy. While we're waiting, can you give me Mr Bracy's address and telephone number. I'd better have both home and work, if you've got them.' He was still writing when the clatter of footsteps announced Rootham's arrival. 'Now off with her clothes, and then we'd like to be left alone.'

This procedure tested even Mr Brogan's bonhomie, and he was very slow about leaving the two men alone in the room. It was a square room, with pink walls and a powder-blue carpet, which was not entirely clean. The air, too, was far from fresh, and the two colleagues looked at each other, neither wishing to start their distasteful examination.

Rootham sighed. 'Heart attack?'

'That's what it says.'

'What first?'

'We'll check for bruises. She clearly hasn't been suffocated.' The two men worked silently.

'Neck okay?'

'Bit stiff still.'

'What now?'

'The dreaded search for injection marks.'

'Let's get on with it.' Rootham took off his jacket. 'What a stench.'

'Just be grateful we didn't have to dig her up.'

'Over she goes.'

'It's funny how flesh goes like this.'

'What's that?'

Proby was staring through a pencil-shaped magnifying glass with its own built-in torch. 'I don't know. No, it's just a mole.'

'Funny place to have one. Did you hear Julie's back?'

'Julie Dart?'

'Yes. She's moved up on to Bert Irwin's squad. Rape support, that sort of thing.'

'That's good.'

Rootham stared across the body at Proby's expressionless face. 'She wrote to me a couple of times while she was down in London,' he said.

'Wrote to me, too,' remarked Proby.

'Did you write back?'

'Hello!' Proby leaned forward, and Rootham moved round the woman's feet to see where he was looking. 'Here, you take a look. Just in the fold of flesh there.'

'Mmm. Ingenious!'

'So.' Proby straightened himself. 'We'd better get Doc Milligan over here sharpish. The sooner this is confirmed, the better.'

'Could have been a painkiller?'

'Injected at the top of the thigh? Bet you a fiver it's insulin.'

'No thanks,' said Rootham. 'It's *always*

insulin. But what's really interesting is this: it looks as if our anonymous caller did know something...'

'We'd better get over there. If she does, whoever she is, she could be in danger too.'

Chapter 19

'Yes?'

'Miss Reid? The Matron?' She seemed far too attractive for such a portentous title. Had he really reached the age when even matrons started getting younger?

'Yes.' She looked at his strong, even aggressive, face with its long nose and delicate cheekbones overpowered by the almost exaggerated breadth of his chin. A Pict, and not one a stray Roman would have wished to meet on a windy Northumbrian night the wrong side of Hadrian's Wall. 'How may I help?'

'This is Ted Rootham,' a slighter man, with signs of a dark evening stubble, and very sharp eyes, 'and I'm Jim Proby.' He held out his warrant card.

'It's not a very good likeness, Inspector,' she said with a slight smile.

'It was taken on a bad day,' his smile was unexpectedly warm. 'May we go to your office? We need to speak in private.'

'Of course.'

As they walked, three abreast, down the corridor, a figure darted across in the half-shadows at the far end.

'Did you see who I saw?' murmured

Rootham out of the corner of his mouth.

'Surely that couldn't have been our old friend Larry Judd?'

'Mr Judd?' said Barbara in surprise. 'Our Head Porter? Do you know him?'

'Yes *indeed*,' said Proby with his imperturbable smile, as Rootham quickened his step and left them to enter the Matron's office without him. 'He's an old friend of ours.'

'Always very cheery,' she commented. 'Never short of a story.'

'You can say that again,' said Proby, seating himself heavily on the more solid-looking chair beside her desk.

'Now?' She laid both her hands flat across the desk. 'What is it?'

There was a defensiveness, a sense of fear almost perfectly concealed, in her eyes which Proby registered while taking out his notepad. 'Mrs Bracy.'

She seemed mightily relieved. 'Mrs Bracy?'

'She died this morning.'

'Yes. She'd been here for several months.'

'I think of this place more as a short-stay acute facility, rather than a long-stay nursing home.'

'And you're quite right. Mrs Bracy came in for a hip replacement, quite routine. But after the usual period of convalescence, it was obvious that she was showing clear signs of accelerating senile dementia.'

'As in Alzheimer's?'

'Well, yes, more or less. They are… yes, for the sake of argument, that's right.'

'So she stayed?'

'Yes. Normally we'd have recommended she be moved to Snarlston Hall, or one of the other longstay nursing home, but…'

'Business is slack?'

'Exactly.'

'How much do you charge per week?'

'Eight hundred guineas.'

Proby pursued his lips. 'And how many people here tonight?'

'Twenty-three.'

'Out of how many beds?'

'Sixty.'

'All single rooms?'

'Of course.'

'Yes. At that rate I imagine they have all the fixings.'

'Quite.'

There was a tap on the door and Rootham, rather red in the face, came in. Proby raised his eyebrows, but the other man shook his head. Mr Judd had clearly eluded his old acquaintance. As he sat down, Proby asked, 'And how were her bills settled?'

'I don't think there's any secret about that,' said Barbara slowly. 'Her nephew Terence signs the cheques. He visits her twice a week. Can you tell me what this is all about?'

Proby crossed his legs. 'We had an anonymous call this afternoon suggesting Mrs Bracy
had been murdered.'

'Oh?' Her quick change of colour might
have been due to the thought of a violent crime,
but both men immediately made the assumption
that she knew the identity of the caller, unless,
indeed, it had been her. Unfortunately the
quality of the recording was not good.

'Would that have been you, Miss Reid?' put
in Rootham aggressively.

'No!' She shook her head vehemently. 'No,
of course not.'

'Can you think of anyone who might have
wanted to murder Mrs Bracy?'

Half a dozen, she thought, starting with me!
But she shook her head. 'I think it sounds most
unlikely. Dr Singh signed the death certificate.
He was perfectly satisfied.'

'I'll need to see him in due course. And
everyone else involved. Tell me why Dr Gresham
didn't sign the certificate himself. I believe he's
the Medical Director here?'

'You really think she was murdered?' The
realization that he was in earnest, and the awful
implications of that, were just beginning to sink
in, and she shivered involuntarily. 'But that…
that's dreadful.'

'We have to follow up these sort of things.
You haven't answered my question.'

'I'm sorry?'

'Dr Gresham.'

'He had to go out unexpectedly. He would normally have dealt with the paperwork, but Dr Singh is perfectly well qualified to act as he did.'

'Who nursed Mrs Bracy?'

She changed colour again. 'We all did. I suppose Nurse O'Neill and Nurse Grant were mainly involved on that corridor. And Nurse Jameson did most of the night duty.'

'What medication was she on?'

'Well, it varied of course. Very little, in fact. There was nothing wrong with her body. It was her mind which was beginning to deteriorate, if you understand me?'

'Perfectly. So what was she taking? Valium? Mogadon?'

'I'll have to consult her case notes, but offhand I would say nothing at all. We used to give her two Temazepam when she had trouble sleeping. But that was fairly unusual.'

'Who was on duty last night?'

'Nurse Grant.'

'And she gave her… what?'

'Nothing!' snapped Barbara. 'Nothing at all.'

'How can you be so sure?' It was Rootham's turn again.

She gazed angrily at his scrubby upper lip. Was he trying to grow a moustache? If so, it was a pathetic result. 'Because,' she said, 'I was here too.'

'Was that usual?' Proby again.

She shrugged. 'It depends.'

'On?'

'How short-handed we are. One of our patients had had a relapse. I wanted to keep an eye on him.'

'Who first discovered that Mrs Bracy was dead?'

'Nurse Grant, when she went to check her.'

'The time?'

'Nine thirty-five.'

'And when had she last seen her alive?'

'You'd be better off asking her that.'

'Fine.' Proby made a great point of placing a big tick against what he had written, as if he was now entirely satisfied, then added, 'And what routine injections would Mrs Bracy be given?' He had brought his voice right down, so that the question came out in the most reassuringly cool tone. He was looking at his notebook, while Rootham's eyes suddenly focused on the carpet. But both men's antennae were concentrated to the maximum to analyse whatever resonance they might retrieve from her voice.

'Injections?' She was clearly startled. 'She would have had no injections. Why do you ask?'

'Purely routine.' Proby smiled at her. 'You have the "Nursing Process", we have "questions-to-be-asked". May I see her room?' There would be plenty of time to ask about the Dispensary and its contents in the course of what looked like being a long evening.

Chapter 20

Dr Singh proved to be a short wiry man, with delicate cheekbones and a slightly satirical slant to his eyebrows. He was almost completely bald.

'Now, Doctor.'

'Yes, Inspector?'

'You examined Mrs Bracy?'

'The woman who died? That is correct.'

'How did you think she had died?'

The doctor tilted his eyebrows. 'A very clear case of myocardial infarction. Heart attack. A merciful release. She was not well in her mind.'

'You had dealt with her before?'

'While she was alive? Yes, from time to time.'

'And?'

'Severe and increasing dementia. She shouldn't have been here, of course. Our wonderful nurses are not really trained for her particular problems.'

'Oh?'

'Well… incontinence, that sort of thing. And she was not an easy lady to nurse.'

'How so?'

The doctor narrowed his fine eyes expressively. 'This is only gossip, naturally. But I heard she made a practice of spying on people. A very malicious old lady, that's what I've heard.'

'Indeed?' Rootham was writing busily. 'Can you give us an example.'

'Ask Mr Judd, the Head Porter. I think she gave him some trouble over something. Why are you asking?'

'There's been a suggestion,' said Proby confidentially, 'that she might have been murdered.'

'*Murdered*!' The doctor's eyes nearly popped out of his head. 'Murdered? And how, I'd like to know? She certainly showed no sign of suffocation, or poisoning. There were no wounds!' He was working himself up into a great state. 'No wounds at all. No bullet holes! No bloody great gashes across the throat!'

'You examined the body?'

'Of course. I signed the certificate, didn't I?'

'Do you normally deal with death certificates here?'

'No.' he said ruefully. 'Never. But Dr Gresham had to go out unexpectedly. And Matron asked me to deal with it. She was very insistent.'

'Would it surprise you to know that I found the mark of an injection at the top of her left thigh?'

There was a long silence while the doctor stared from one policeman to the other. 'Well,' he said at last. 'I don't remember seeing that. But then I wasn't looking for one. But surely to goodness it could have been anything – she might have been given something to make her sleep.'

'Perhaps that's it,' said Proby soothingly. 'I just wanted to check if you had noticed it.'

'I want a solicitor,' said the doctor suddenly. 'I don't wish to continue with this interrogation. I'm not feeling well.'

'That's quite all right,' said Proby, with a wink to Rootham. 'We've no more questions at this time. We're seeing Nurse Grant next. Please will you tell Dr Gresham I'd be grateful if he could spare me a few minutes in, say, half an hour?'

'Certainly, Inspector.' The doctor had a new and rather more serious air about him now. He held open the door for them and then marched off in the direction of Dr Gresham's office, his heels smacking the linoleum with rhythmic precision.

Hannah Grant, trembling with apprehension, was waiting for them in the committee room, a brightly lit space created behind the operating theatre and richly furnished with a long mahogany table and matching heavily carved chairs. She stood up when they entered, giving Rootham an electrifying glimpse of her legs.

'It's Hannah, isn't it?' said Proby kindly. She smiled and nodded. 'Thank you for calling us.' She started and turned so pink that denial would have been pointless. 'Tell me why you believed Mrs Bracy was murdered.' He sat back and examined her. She really was very pretty, with her big dark eyes and wide scared mouth.

'I'm sorry.' Her voice was so low as to be almost inaudible.

'Don't worry, luv,' put in Rootham. 'That's what we're here for.' He beamed at her, turning back to his notes on catching sight of Proby's raised eyebrow.

'It was only to gct back at Dr Grcsham.' As soon as she spoke, she realized she had opened another potentially deeper hole for herself and took refuge in a flood of tears. Either man, alone, might have been tempted to give her the benefit of a comforting arm. Together, they remained impassively seated, waiting.

'Why was that then?' said Proby softly.

'He's a sexist bastard,' she said, recollecting in time that she had more than one reason to hate her employer. 'Always fondling me and making filthy suggestions. I wanted to make trouble for him, that's all.' She raised her eyes, and noted the entirely favourable effect. *Men*! But then, who's knocking it?

'So you had no reason for believing it to be true?' It was the older man who spoke. He liked her, that was plain enough, but the younger man was just gasping for it. In fact, he looked rather dishy himself. That was one of the nicest things about Hannah Grant; she loved giving people a good time.

'No, of course not,' she said confidingly.

'The old bag had a heart attack, didn't she?'

'I want to go through the events of the night,' said Proby, and noted a wary look returning to her eyes. What on earth went on in this hospital, that they all had so much to hide? 'You settled her down at, what, ten o'clock?'

'Yes. I took her some cocoa. She liked a hot drink last thing.'

'Did she drink it?'

'No! She threw it against the wall, as per usual.'

'What then?'

'I cleaned it up, and left her to it.'

'Nothing to help her sleep?'

'Not till later. Her bell went about half-past eleven. She said she couldn't sleep. She was swearing like a fishwife saying it was all my fault. I got her a glass of water and gave her two capsules, as specified in Dr Gresham's notes.'

'Temazepam?'

She stared at him. 'That's right.'

'She swallowed them?'

'I made damn sure she did.'

'And you went back to the nurses' station.'

'Yes.' A lie, he noted. The first one. Why?

'Did you get any sleep?'

'Yes. Matron was on duty too, so I had a couple of hours on the dayroom couch.'

'And you found her dead?'

She shuddered. 'Yes. It's not the first time, of course. But it always gets to me. I took her in some tea at half-past nine. I knew she was dead straight away.'

'How so?'

'The way she was lying. The stillness. You can tell.' If the two men agreed, they weren't telling.

'Nine-thirty seems late for a morning call?' queried Proby.

'Not for Mrs Bracy,' she said. 'If you woke her too early, she'd throw everything everywhere.'

'You don't sound as if you liked her.'

'I didn't.'

'And you've been on duty all day too?'

'Oh no. I went off-duty after handing over to the day shift. I came back about an hour ago.' She certainly looked fresh and alert.

'You live very near then,' put in Rootham.

She opened her eyes wide at him. 'How do you know that?'

'Elementary, Miss Grant. You rang from that callbox just across the street.'

She grinned, showing sharp little teeth. 'Yeh. There's a nurses' lodging there. It's very nice.'

'I'm sure it is,' agreed Rootham, almost purring.

Had he really detected an invitation? That was the best part of this job, the people you get to meet.

'Are you licensed to give injections?' asked Proby.

'Of course. I'm a registered nurse.'

'What injections did Mrs Bracy routinely receive?'

'None.' she said decisively. 'She was as fit as a fiddle, apart from her brain.'

'A bit of a nosey-parker, I've heard,' murmured Proby.

'Bloody blackmailer more like,' said Hannah incautiously before blushing again. Rootham gazed at her with undisguised admiration, her hair, her eyes, her voice, her…

'Sergeant, would you mind getting us all some water. It's getting very stuffy in here.' Proby was becoming impatient, a bad sign. Rootham got up quickly.

'Just down the hall.' breathed Hannah, with an encouraging smile.

'Thanks,' muttered Rootham, his head well down. 'I'll find it.'

'Blackmailing in what way?'

She shook her head. 'I'm sorry. That was a silly exaggeration. She just couldn't help being malicious about everything.'

Another lie, but one that could wait. 'Now, Hannah.' said Proby. 'I want to know about the other patients. Who else have you got in?'

'Well' she put her head on one side. 'There's Mr van Oss with chronic high blood pressure, Mrs Tentercroft with a broken arm, Colonel Bridgeman with his varicose veins, poor man, and Mrs Rigby recuperating after a hysterectomy. That's my corridor. There are lots of others on the other floors of course.'

'No one with diabetes?'

She stared at him. 'No,' she said. 'Why do you ask?'

'Is Colonel Bridgeman an elderly man with a very fine moustache?'

She giggled. 'Yes,' she said, nodding her head. 'It has a life of its own. Do you know him?'

'I've met him,' said Proby. 'Now, on to a different topic. Thank you.' Rootham had returned with a tray complete with three glasses of water and a jug. He looked excited about something. Proby raised his eyebrows but Rootham shook his head. Whatever it was could evidently wait. 'I presume you keep the medicines locked away?'

She nodded again. 'Each corridor has its own dispensary.'

'Who has the keys?'

'Matron, the doctors, and the senior nurse on duty for each floor.'

'Is that you?'

'Yes.'

'Are there any circumstances when the door would be left unlocked?'

'Oh no!' she said vehemently. 'Never.'

'May we see it?' He stood up, but she remained seated, staring up at him.

'It was only a stupid hoax,' she said. 'I don't really think the old cow was murdered. You're wasting your time.'

'We don't think so,' said Proby repressively. 'Now lead us to this well-secured dispensary.'

He let her walk on ahead before turning to Rootham, 'Well?'

'Guess who I saw parked in a car across the street?' 'Parked in a car?'

'Yes. He lit a cigarette. I spotted him from the galley window. Grimshaw.'

'Drug Squad?'

'Yeh. I reckon he's watching one of our doctors. Like you told them to.'

'That's an interesting idea.'

'Here we are.' Hannah took out a big ring of keys and inserted one to unlock the heavy door. It had a ventilation grille and as soon as she opened it, a light inside flashed and came on, illuminating row upon row of medical supplies, all neatly arranged.

'Is there a ledger?'

'Of course.' She handed him a heavy book with a Biro attached to it by a piece of frayed orange twine.

'Let's have a look.' He laid it on the counter and pored over its largely incomprehensible hieroglyphics. 'Whose signature is that?'

'That's Matron's.'

'And that?'

'Dr Gresham's.'

'I'm interested in insulin.'

'Why?' She put out a hand to steady herself.

'Because I'm expecting a call from Doctor Milligan any minute to say that the post-mortem suggests Mrs Bracy was poisoned with insulin.'

'I can't believe it. That's terrible.'

'Yes.' He looked down at her sternly. 'Now I'm to have a word with Dr Gresham. I want you to talk to my sergeant here, and tell him all about Mrs Bracy. Particularly on the subject of blackmail. And this time, Miss Grant, I want the truth.'

Chapter 21

He could hear them shouting from the other end of the corridor. They must have been at it for more than twenty minutes. He rapped on the door.

'Who is it?' A rasping, angry voice.

'Dr Gresham?'

The door was flung open to reveal a heavy man with blotched cheeks, wild hair and bloodshot eyes. His breath stank of alcohol. 'What is it?'

'I'm Detective Inspector Proby. I think Dr Singh,' he peered round the door to where the other doctor, his bare scalp scarlet from his exertions, was shaking with fury, 'may have told you I was coming to see you.'

'Yes.' Dr Gresham wiped his mouth. 'Yes, of course. Dr Singh and I have finished our discussion.' He glowered at his colleague, who took a step forward, as if to assault him, and then brushed past Proby, muttering something under his breath. 'Do come in.'

'Thank you. As I expect you know, I am investigating a possible crime in connection with the death of Mrs Elizabeth Bracy.'

'Nonsense. She died in her sleep.'

'Yes,' agreed Proby. 'That seems entirely likely. The question is, how did she die?'

'Heart attack.'

'That is possible. I'm rather hoping Dr Milligan is carrying out the post-mortem as we speak. That will confirm it one way or another.'

'What I don't see,' said Dr Gresham slowly, 'is why the police are involved in the first place.'

'Just routine,' said Proby. 'You were treating Bracy?'

'After a fashion. There wasn't much wrong with her. She was just very confused, mentally.'

'What medication did you prescribe?'

'Nothing.' He was rubbing his temples in a circular fashion. 'I'm sorry if I seem abrupt. I've got a terrible headache.'

'I see.' Proby examined his notes. 'She was given Temazepam to help her sleep?'

'One or two capsules, nothing dangerous about that.'

'Injections?'

'No. Why?'

'Tell me about the death certificate?'

'What about it?'

'The body was discovered at... er... thirty-five?'

'About then. I checked her, of course, and confirmed the nurses' opinion that she was dead.'

'How long?'

'Good heavens!' Dr Gresham stood up in his agitation. 'Why should I have bothered with that? She died of a heart attack. There was some rigor, of course.' He was trying to control himself. 'If I had to guess, I should say she died around three.'

The red telephone on his desk began to ring. He snatched it up. 'I don't want to be disturbed... who? Oh.' He handed the receiver to Proby, who listened carefully.

'I'm very grateful to you,' he said after a while. 'Yes, would you? Can you give me even an approximate time of death? She took the capsules at twenty-three thirty.' He waited again. 'I see. Thanks.' He handed the receiver back to Dr Gresham.

'Well? I assume that was the result of the post-mortem?'

Proby nodded. 'Her blood-sugar level was as near nought per cent as makes no difference, consistent, as I'm sure you know, with someone having injected two millilitres of insulin into her bloodstream. Milligan can't give me much guidance on time of death, but says the Temazepam was almost entirely absorbed. Three a.m. sounds like a fair guess. That suggests to me she was given the insulin around midnight. Would you agree?' But Dr Gresham was speechless, his mouth clamped shut, and drops of perspiration were running down his forehead. 'Excuse me,' he said, and ran for a door at the back of the office. Proby listened with distaste to the sound of the doctor vomiting.

The sound of a lavatory flushing followed, and then running water. 'I'm sorry.' His hair was dripping wet. He must have plunged his head into a basin. 'I feel better now.'

'Good.'

'This is unbelievable.'

'I spotted the mark of the injection myself.'

'I saw nothing.'

'Evidently,' said Proby drily. 'Now, I want to go back to the death certificate. You were saying that you made a cursory examination, and satisfied yourself that Mrs Bracy was dead. You were her doctor while she was here. Why didn't you sign the certificate yourself?'

Dr Gresham shrugged. 'Well,' he said, 'I had to go out. An urgent call.' Proby sighed. Another lie! Was no one in this building able to tell him the truth?

'Do you mind telling me where you went?'

Dr Gresham stared at him. 'Yes,' he said. 'I do mind. It's confidential, and can have no bearing on this case.'

'I'd rather decide that for myself.'

'I'm not prepared to break medical confidentiality.' The atmosphere in the room had abruptly changed. The doctor's voice crackled with something. Anger? Or fear? And there was a stubborn obstructive set to his face.

'Perhaps you need a solicitor too?' suggested Proby with a nasty smile.

'Why?' He was panicking again. 'I want to help you. Of course, I do. This is terrible news for my business. I couldn't have killed her. I had every reason to want her to stay alive.'

'One of your best customers?'

'Precisely!'

'It's been suggested she was involved in blackmail.'

'*Blackmail*. Mrs Bracy?' The idea evidently struck him as preposterous.

'You doubt that?'

'I certainly do. She was just an old lady with incipient Alzheimer's.'

'She never tried to blackmail you, then?'

The smile was a shade too quick. 'No! Of course not. What on earth about?'

'Indeed. I'd like some space here to set up an Incident Room, and access to all your personnel files. How long has your Head Porter been here?'

'Judd? He's been here nearly three years. A very dependable fellow. Great sense of humour. You can have this office if you like.'

'That would be excellent, but I need a little more space.'

Dr Gresham smiled. 'There's a lumber room next door. That used to be an office too. If Matron doesn't object, I'm sure you could use that.

'I'll ask her,' said Proby, noting the other's malicious smirk. 'Now I'd like to see the other nurses.'

Chapter 22

'James Arthur Proby?'

He grunted his assent. It was seven the next morning, and he hadn't even had time to shave. There were press photographers everywhere, and he could see old Mrs Tighe next door grinning from behind her lace curtains. Bloody old bat!

The bailiff handed him the summons. 'Sorry, Jim,' he muttered. 'Especially about this circus.'

'You can buy me a pint, Ned. If I get off.' Both men exchanged covert smiles.

'Jim! This way!'

'Over here, Inspector! Just one more.'

He showed them an impassive, grave exterior, as befitted a man accused of a very serious crime. He didn't want any headlines along the lines of 'Policeman laughs at justice' or 'Proby chuckles all the way to the court'.

'Good luck, Jim.' He recognized the voice of George Pratt, the local crime reporter, but still maintained his serious expression. 'Thank you, George,' he said.

'Don't let the buggers get you down!' This from his other neighbour, Fred Harston. 'Here! Clear off out of my garden!'

Proby slipped back inside his house, and slammed the door.

'Who was it?'

'Bloody bailiff. With my court summons. Here you are: "... that the said James Arthur Proby did murder James Creasey on the seventh of October 1994." Can you believe that?' She shook her head silently. 'I mean...' His voice faltered, and, shocked, she ran to him and hugged him as hard as she could.

'Just be yourself,' she said. 'I believe in you, and so do all your friends. Everyone you respect believes in you.'

'That's a comfort,' he said, smiling again. What he didn't say was that he wasn't entirely certain whether he believed in himself.

He was at his desk by eight, reading through the detailed post-mortem report and checking that statements were being taken from every member of staff and every patient at the Hampton Clinic. There had been another alleged sighting of the missing driver, this time in Tadcaster, and he sent Braithwaite and Oates over in a car to interview the people involved. It would take them most of the day, but it would give the Chief something positive to say in his next press release.

At eight forty-five, Rankin looked in. 'Any sign of your brief?'

'I believe he's coming up on the London

train. Due in now in fact. The solicitor is waiting downstairs.'

'Police Federation bod?'

'All bought and paid for.'

'Glad they do something for us. I'll walk over with you when it's time. I suppose they will give you bail?'

'Well if not, you'll have to put White in charge of the Bracy case.'

'What about this one?'

'I think you should handle that yourself.'

'Oh God!' groaned the other. 'I was hoping to get away next week.'

'Well, all you've got to do is make sure they do give me bail. Lean on the magistrates. Threaten to audit their expenses. You'll think of something.' Rankin grinned. 'I'll be back.'

'See you.'

Ten minutes later he was summoned to one of the conference rooms where his solicitor, Mr Michaels, introduced him to the London barrister, Tufton Drage. They looked more like a music hall turn than a needle-sharp legal team ready to overthrow the opposition. Where Michaels was thin, skinny even, with tufts of sparse grey hair, vague eyes and a nose almost as long as Proby's, Drage was a pure suet pudding, with a bulging belly, colourless flabby face, and plastered down hair. His lips were large and red, and he had cut himself quite badly, shaving under his stubby little nose. A piece of stained cottonwool gave the misleading impression of half a white moustache. Both men wore ill-fitting black suits.

'Come in, Jim.' muttered Michaels, looking at the floor. 'This is Mr Drage.'

'Thank you for coming at such short notice,' said Proby politely.

'It was rather inconvenient,' said the barrister. 'But it's a very important case. Striking as it does at the root of law-enforcement.'

'We haven't much time,' interjected Michaels looking at his watch.

'Let me just go through my notes,' said Drage. 'Your story is that he slipped from your grasp while you were trying to rescue him, absurd if every time you try to save someone you're had up for murder, de-dah-de-dah-de-dah?'

'More or less,' acknowledged Proby with a smile.

'Let's hope it's more,' grunted Drage, 'because I'd hate to be taking the case if it were less! I'm going to try for bail of course.'

'Try? I'm in the middle of two murder cases!' said Proby.

'And you don't want to be banged up with all your old chums, eh?' Michaels sniggered, oblivious of Proby's scowl since he was now gazing at the ceiling.

'Joking apart,' said Drage, fingering the cottonwool, 'it's quite unusual to grant bail in a murder case.'

'Even when there's no evidence?'

'Well, you did drop the man, there's no getting away from that. Come on.' Drage winked slowly at him, a strangely aggressive gesture wholly devoid of goodwill. 'Let's meet the magistrates.' He heaved himself out of his chair.

Chapter 23

There was more media madness outside the little courthouse, with arc lights, and men on step-ladders jostling for position. Proby's case seemed more to the taste of the country's tabloids than Mrs Bracy's suspicious death, or even the original murdering of four innocent citizens in the course of the post office robbery.

'*How does it feel like to have your OWN collar felt?*'

'We thought you might have an overcoat over your head!' shouted another. Proby brushed aside the thrusting microphones with his habitual stolid courtesy, and pushed his way through the faded swing doors and into the dank little lobby. To his amazement, the Chief Constable was there, chatting to Mr Rankin and two of the other Superintendents.

He came over to shake hands. 'Good luck, Jim.' It seemed entirely sincere.

'Thank you, sir.'

'We're all behind you.' Surely not even Chief Superintendent Knowles from Traffic!

'I'm very grateful.'

'We can't do without you! Get in there and give them hell.' There was a lot of good-humoured laughter.

'Sorry, Jim.' It was the Court Usher, a sheepish look on his usually cheerful face. 'This way please.' As he passed through the low door into the courtroom, and saw Sheila's strained smile from the gallery above, he began to appreciate the real threat of his position for the first time. A fine way to end his career, doing life in Parkhurst!

'James Arthur Proby.' He was tempted to pinch himself to be certain he was actually now standing in this same battered mahogany dock, which had circumscribed the previously uninhibited movements of old acquaintances such as Leo 'Socks' Nucci, Matthews the Jewgate Rapist and Hippo Doyle. 'You are charged that you did, on Friday the seventh day of October, 1994, murder James Creasey.' A nice simple indictment. No frills. 'How do you plead?'

He glanced at his watch. Ten minutes past ten. Rootham should be questioning Terence Bracy, not sitting up there next to Sheila, with that silly frightened grin on his face. Hadn't the man got a job to do?

'I said,' repeated the voice, 'how do you plead?' A profound silence had settled on the murky room. The silent preoccupation of the man in the dock had electrified the onlookers. He couldn't be going to plead *guilty*, could he?

Proby looked up. 'Not guilty,' he said, in a loud clear voice. Everyone sat back, relaxing, except for the elderly barrister, Mr Gregory, whose unusual job it was to present the private prosecution ostensibly on behalf of James Creasey's half-brother, but funded by 'The Citizens for Safety'. Mr Gregory had a cold, as usual, and had already used up his one pocket handkerchief leaving him no choice but to rely on the Court lavatory's pink tissues. He wiped his nose miserably and swallowed hard, before rising to his feet to address the magistrates. They did not look entirely receptive.

In the chair, a tall lean woman in her early forties with thick tortoiseshell spectacles, was watching his damp piece of tissue with open disgust, her lips drawn back in a rictus of nausea. On her right an elderly man seemed to be already nodding off, his eyes half-closed and his head drooping, while on her left, taking a sip from her glass of water, a short round woman with dyed red curls was apparently winking at the accused. It certainly hadn't been his idea to pursue the policeman, but he was glad of the fees and determined to make a success of it. Perhaps he could found a new career prosecuting policemen all over the island. There were plenty who deserved it!

'Madam Chairman,' he said, sniffing hard. 'I am prosecuting this case, and my learned colleague Mr Drage appears for the defence. I shall be asking you to remand the prisoner until a date can be set for his trial, and will be presenting the evidence on which to base this judgement.' He bowed and sat down.

Mr Drage rose. 'I appear for the accused, Madam Chairman, and I shall be asking you to dismiss the case on the grounds of lack of evidence. Failing that, I shall be asking you to release my client on bail.'

'In a murder case, Mr Drage?' The presiding magistrate adjusted her glasses and stared at him. 'Isn't that a trifle *unusual*?'

'It's a very unusual case, Madam Chairman,' he replied with an unctuous smile, which she chose to ignore. It was plain that London barristers held little appeal to gritty Hampton magistrates.

'Then we'd better hear it, hadn't we? Mr Gregory, please!' she snapped, discreetly poking her elderly neighbour in the ribs with a devastating forefinger. The poor old man's mouth flew open in silent protest, but he did make a visible effort to sit up straight and concentrate.

'Madam Chairman,' Mr Gregory fixed her with his most solemn expression. 'It gives me no pleasure to be prosecuting a senior officer of the Hampton police force for so grave an offence as murder. We, all of us, look to the police as our first, indeed, I may say, principal, bulwark against the encroachment of crime, the creeping cancer that threatens the very heart of our society, the insidious growth...'

'Mr Gregory!'

'Yes, Madam Chairman?' He made no

attempt to conceal his irritation at being interrupted in full flood.

'This is a magistrates' court. There is no jury to impress. I realize that the press are here in force,' she glowered round at the scribbling hacks, 'but we have a formidable workload today and we will get on faster if you can present your case with as little embroidery as possible.'

'I am deeply grateful, Madam Chairman,' he said. 'I don't wish to delay this Court's workload in any way unnecessarily, but if you will allow me to go about it in my own way, I feel we will get along to your satisfaction. This is a case of national, nay, international importance. But I will endeavour to be as brief as my duty to justice permits.'

'Pray do so,' said the magistrate frostily, 'if you wish to be assured of our fullest attention.'

'Quite so. As I was saying, to coin a phrase, "*Quis custodiet ipsos custodes?*"...'

'Mr Gregory!' He smiled beatifically up at her, and raised his eyebrows very high. 'For the benefit of those few here who do not regularly converse in the Latin tongue, might we agree to stick to good plain English?'

'To put it another way,' he continued imperturbably, 'who will guard us from the guards themselves?' He stared round at the journalists. 'Who indeed! The facts of this case are very simple, and will be amply confirmed should the defence take the morally courageous course of calling the defendant to the dock…'

'Madam Chairman!' Mr Drage had bobbed up from his seat with a screech of wounded outrage.

'Yes, Mr Drage?'

'I must protest. I am, just, willing to accept my learned friend's lamentable attempts to impress us with his dog Latin, but I must object to his unwarrantable intrusion into the conduct of the case for the defence.'

She nodded vigorously. 'I entirely agree. Please confine yourself to presenting your own case, Mr Gregory. We won't get very far if you're relying on the defendant to supply your evidence.'

Mr Gregory bowed low again. 'James Creasey, an exemplary soldier recently made redundant under the present Government's "New Model Army" policy, found himself unexpectedly the subject of intense pursuit by armed men, who, as we know now, were members of the Hampton constabulary. Seeking to evade a potentially alarming confrontation, he tried to descend from the top of the Gull Insurance building using a rope sling. During this testing manoeuvre, something went sadly wrong.

'Exactly what, we will never now know. Mr Creasey's untimely death has left this episode in the whole sorry story forever shrouded in impenetrable mystery. We may speculate, we may advance theoretical explanations as to why James

Creasey came to be hanging by his very fingertips from the roof of that building, but we can never,' his voice had shrunk to a conspiratorial whisper, 'be sure.'

Noting the magistrate's gathering frown, he hurried on. 'There he was, hanging on for dear life, when Detective Inspector Proby, who stands before you in the dock, heard his frantic appeals for help. Now!' He raised one finger in a dramatic flourish. 'The defendant had not paused for thought since finding one of his own officers, a fine policeman with many years' service behind him, butchered on the floor below. Did he leap to the, perhaps pardonable, assumption that this young man suspended in mid-air was indeed the assassin? Perhaps he will tell us. But he had no shred of proof beyond geographical propinquity, to back up such an assumption. And, Madam Chairman, he holds no commission, neither explicit nor inferred, to act as judge, jury, or executioner in the case. His job, as a policeman, is to apprehend a suspect, using no more than reasonable force. There, and precisely there, his role ends. It is for others to decide on guilt and, where appropriate, punishment.

'Now, Madam Chairman, we know two further facts: we know that Inspector Proby leaned over, ostensibly to assist this young man, and we know that James Creasey, in the prime of life, was shortly thereafter found with the life

cruelly crushed out of him at the foot of that
immense building. It is the prosecution's case
that the defendant, blind with anger at the death
of his colleague, and confused by the fury of the
chase as to the identity of Mr Creasey, took hold
of this man's hands, stretched up to him in the
extremity of his danger, and then, forsaking his
duty as an officer of the law, deliberately dropped
him onto the concrete far below. You, Madam
Chairman, and your fellow magistrates, will know
that it matters not one jot whether James Creasey
subsequently might have been implicated in the
robbery or in the aforesaid murders. If the defendant, a heavily built man, deliberately or even
with an unreasonable recklessness encouraged
James Creasey to leave go his hold on the
building, entrusting himself to his apparent
rescuer, and then let him fall, he is without any
doubt guilty of murder.' Gregory sat down with a
heavy thump.

The three magistrates conferred. 'Mr
Gregory?'

'Yes, Madam Chairman?'

'You don't seem to be calling any witnesses?'

'No, ma'am. You have there the whole of the
case for the prosecution.'

She raised her eyebrows. 'That's *it*?'

'That's it.'

'Mr Drage?' The defending barrister heaved
his outsized body onto its legs and wiped his
upper lip. 'Are you ready to present your case

against committal?'

He smiled at her. 'Madam Chairman, in any other case than this,, I would invite Your Worships to dismiss the case forthwith. This infamous private prosecution, funded, as is common knowledge, by a fringe group of the most dubious origins, not unconnected…'

'I don't think we need concern ourselves with that, do you?'

'Perhaps not. Howsoever…' but he had lost the thread of his argument, and, the cottonwool having come away from his lip, the razor nick was beginning to distract him by releasing a dribble of blood onto his lip. 'Er…' Vainly he shuffled his papers while everyone in the Court watched him. Proby, his palms sweating now, saw DC Allan walk into the gallery and approach Rootham. The two men whispered together, with increasing intensity, and then both rose and tiptoed out of the room, though not before Rootham had flashed him a sympathetic and apologetic smile. 'The point, Madam Chairman…' Drage had recovered his fragile aplomb, 'is that in any other case, I would simply be asking you to dismiss this shoddy case with the contempt it deserves. Howsoever, the reputation of a fine policeman, a man I might go so far as to characterize as a pillar of the law-abiding community of this proud city and county, has been put needlessly and maliciously at risk. Justice must not only be done, but must be seen to be done.' Did the man actually want him put on trial? Was it then just a question of extra fees? Proby stared at his defender with increasing unease. 'I shall therefore call,' declaimed Drage, swelling his voice with rhetorical splendour, 'Detective Inspector James Proby to give public evidence in his own defence.'

They had never even discussed this! But why not? Proby found himself automatically adjusting his tie as he walked to the witness box and took the oath.

'You are James Arthur Proby, of seventeen, Church View, Graceby?' Drage bathed him in an oily smile.

'I am.'

'And you hold the rank of Detective Inspector in the Hampton Police Force?'

'I do.'

'I want to stick to the simple details of this tragic accident, as tragic for you as for the late Mr Creasey. On reaching the roof of the Gull building, you heard a cry for help?'

Mr Gregory rose. 'Madam Chairman!'

'Yes,' intervened the senior magistrate. 'Mr Drage! Allow the Inspector to tell his own story without leading him.'

'Let me put it another way,' said Drage. 'When you reached the roof of the Gull building, did you hear anything?'

'Yes,' said Proby stolidly. 'A cry for help.' Mr Gregory rolled his eyes at the nearest journalist, who obligingly made a note.

'Just tell us what happened in your own words.'

'Well.' Proby closed his eyes. It wasn't that he hadn't thought about the memories before. It was precisely because he *had* thought about them too much. 'I heard this voice. There was an automatic weapon lying on the edge of the roof and the voice seemed to be coming from that direction. I crawled to the edge, and looked over.'

'That must have taken a bit of doing,' said the elderly magistrate, suddenly coming to life, and just as abruptly quelled by a look from his Chairman. 'Please go on,' she said courteously.

'Yes, well...' He paused. 'Sergeant Rootham and another officer were holding my legs, so that I couldn't topple over. And there he was, just three or four feet, the length of his arms, below me.'

'What were your feelings?'

'It gave me quite a fright.' There was just the fleeting suggestion of a giggle or two from the press benches, hastily stifled.

'I imagine it did. What then?'

'He was clinging onto a bit of the building.'

'In imminent danger of failing?'

'Yes. I should say so, yes.'

'And?'

'I reached down.' Proby's eyes were almost squinting with the effort. 'I got one of his hands.'

'To pull him up?'

'Of course.' The whole room was breathless,

with Proby's face the focus of all their staring eyes.

'Did he speak?'

'He said: "Help me." I told him to give me his other hand. And then... then he was gone.'

'You tried to save him?'

'Yes.'

'You didn't decide to become, what was it, "judge, jury and executioner"?'

'No.'

'You risked your life to save a man, but without success?' Proby paused, then nodded. Mr Gregory, who had noted the pause, wrote something on his pad and passed it back to his instructing solicitor who was crouched on the bench behind. The man read the note, and grinned maliciously.

'Most people would call you a hero?'

'No,' said Proby, almost angrily. 'I was doing my job.'

'Your job in protecting the citizens of Hampton, precisely.' Mr Drage sat down, with much ceremony, as if his day's work was done.

'Inspector Proby?' Mr Gregory had risen for the cross-examination with a wintry look in his eyes. 'How long have you been a member of this force?'

'Thirty-two years, sir.'

'Really? And how long have you been a Detective Inspector?'

'Nineteen years.'

'Nineteen years? That must be almost some kind of record, mustn't it? I should have thought a man of your obvious talents would have risen far higher in the ranks by now?'

'Perhaps so.'

'So can you explain to the Court why you have remained at this rank for *nineteen years?*'

Proby gave him a sad smile. 'I've never sought promotion,' he said.

'Ah, but have you actually turned it down?' sneered Mr Gregory.

'Yes, sir,' said Proby quietly.

Mr Gregory stared. 'And why was that?'

Proby could see his senior officers sitting in a phalanx of official probity, all staring down at him now. He grinned. 'I prefer to work on the ground,' he explained. 'It's where I feel most at ease. I'm not much good at desk-work.'

'Tell me,' said Mr Gregory with an insidious little smile, 'apart from this case before us today, have you ever killed a man?' Drage made as if to rise and protest, but something in Proby's face made him hesitate, and join the rest of the men and women in the courtroom, staring at the rugged man in the witness stand.

Proby's face had changed completely. Gone was the homely image of the avuncular bobby on the beat, the caring copper. The skin had tightened round his eyes, and his lips were strained back from his teeth, so that they seemed bared against the world. 'Yes,' he said slowly. 'I have had to kill in the course of my job.'

'One man? Two?' Mr Gregory could scarcely believe his good fortune. '*Three?*' So excited was he by this lucky shot in the dark that he was teetering on the balls of his feet.

Proby shook his head. 'Not three men. Three men and a woman.' he said flatly. Even the magistrates looked startled. Had they stumbled upon a new serial killer? 'The Mad Inspector of Hampton'?

'*Three men and a woman*? You seem to live in exciting times in Hampton,' said Mr Gregory with a significant look at the press.

'It gives me no pleasure to talk about it,' growled Proby. 'Rather the reverse.' Indeed the public perception of this man had altered, significantly, in the last few moments. Suddenly he seemed a man to be feared, a man experienced in dealing out death, for whatever reason.

'Well, well. Be that as it may, I want to turn now to the events on the roof. You thought Mr Creasey had murdered Constable Hickock, didn't you?'

What could Proby say? He certainly had thought that, and he'd been proved right by Forensic since. 'Yes,' he said 'I did think that.'

'Was that why you dropped him?'

Proby stared at Mr Gregory. 'No,' he said.

'So why did you drop him?' This was the nub of the trial, of Proby's ordeal, of the terrible internal dilemma he had wrestled with during the intervening days and nights. He was no fool, and had no wish to be sent to prison for a crime he hadn't committed, nor even for one that he had. But he did wish to tell the truth, and, try as he might, he couldn't truly remember the exact circumstances of the man's fall. Had he dropped him deliberately? Had the man's hands slipped through his? That damned helicopter had been making such a racket!

'I didn't drop him,' he said with a sigh, a sigh which the onlookers translated as the natural impatience of a man of (terrifying) action, but which in fact sprang from dissatisfaction with himself. He raised his eyes and met Sheila's unfathomable gaze. What was she thinking? She had been no stranger to the rougher side of life, yet she could hardly have expected to spend her life with a suburban man so steeped in blood.

'You were angry about Constable Hickock!'

'Certainly.'

'You held in your hands the man who had slaughtered him!'

'I believed so, yes.'

'And you decided to take revenge!'

Slowly, Proby shook his head. 'No,' he said. 'It is not my job to take vengeance.'

'No, it is not!' shouted Mr Gregory, as if to emphasize an important confession. 'Now, in your evidence, you stated, and I'm reading your exact words: "then he was gone". That's what you said?'

'I think so.'

'I assure you that is so. "He was gone".'

'Yes.'

'You're a strong man.'

'Yes'

'You go to a gym?'

'Yes.'

'Once, twice a week?'

'Twice a week.'

'Mr Creasey was quite a small man, wasn't he?'

'Yes'

Mr Gregory leaned forward. 'So how did he go? Tell us that!'

Proby shook his head. 'He just sort of slipped. We were both sweating. There was a lot of noise and wind from the helicopter overhead. I had him quite secure, I thought, and then he was gone.'

'Three hundred and twenty feet onto concrete.'

'Yes,' said Proby. 'It was dreadful.'

'For him!' sneered Mr Gregory.

'I know.' Proby bowed his head. It probably seemed staged and 'insincere, yet it was an entirely genuine impulse of contrition.

'Let me go through the preceding events again…' Mr Gregory was determined to leave nothing unexplored. While the repetitive examination continued, Proby was momentarily distracted by the sight of Rootham returning,

Rootham with a broad triumphant smile, Rootham giving him both thumbs up. What now?

At last Mr Gregory, satisfied that he had extracted every ounce of damaging evidence from Proby, sat down, and Drage rose to re-examine.

'One point needs clarification, Inspector,' he said unctuously. 'These men and this woman whom you were forced to confront and, in the ultimate analysis, kill…?'

'Yes?'

'Am I not right in saying that in each case this was in the process of pursuit and arrest, and that in all cases the coroner's verdict was justifiable homicide?'

Proby stared at him, remembering. 'Yes,' he said softly. 'Yes.'

After an adjournment for lunch, which for Proby took the form of a polystyrene cup of coffee and two cheese sandwiches in a bare cell, the crowd in the Court rose to their feet as the three magistrates returned to their dais. The senior magistrate adjusted her glasses. 'Well,' she said. 'We can continue… but where is Mr Gregory?' Of the shambling old barrister, there was, indeed, no sign.

'Madam Chairman.' It was Marion Darby, the grey-haired woman from the Crown Prosecution Service, clutching a very large briefcase to her ample midriff. 'I have come straight from the

Attorney General and,' she was rummaging in the bag, 'I have here the relevant certificate. The Attorney General has taken over the prosecution on behalf of the Crown. He hereby enters a *nolle prosequi*...' The chief magistrate raised her eyes to the ceiling. 'That is, he will be offering no evidence against Detective Inspector Proby.'

'No evidence?'

'No.'

The senior magistrate conferred with her colleagues. 'In that case, we have great pleasure in releasing Inspector Proby from the case. As the press are still with us,' they were indeed, and scribbling busily, 'I should like, on behalf of my colleagues and myself,' all three were beaming at a bemused Proby, 'to say how much we have regretted the bringing of this case, and to ask the press to record our heartfelt appreciation of his many years of sterling efforts on behalf of our community.'

'Well done thou good and faithful servant, eh?' muttered the man from the *Guardian* to George Pratt beside him. 'Go out and kill another half dozen!' Seeing the magistrate's icy glance turning towards him, he buried his head in his notebook. There was an outburst of clapping from the gallery, where Proby could see Sheila weeping uncontrollably on Rootham's shoulder, while Mr Rankin was gingerly offering her the yellow paisley silk handkerchief from his top pocket.

Chapter 24

'Back to work,' said Proby, trying to disengage himself from all the congratulatory hands that were shaking, patting, slapping and stroking him like some prize dog. 'Ted! Give me the results on the nephew.'

Rootham smirked. 'All wrapped up, guv. Charged, confessed, the works.' The younger man was almost jumping up and down in his jubilation.

'What do you mean?' demanded Proby angrily, forgetting how annoyed he'd been when his subordinate took time off from the case to support him in court.

'Just that. With you busy elsewhere, I thought I'd better get on with it. I just followed your usual course, asked myself who benefited.'

'The nephew, of course.'

'Of course. So I got a search warrant. He'd hidden the insulin bottle and the syringe in a drain-grating right there in his shop's back courtyard.'

'Where'd he get it?'

'Where do you think?'

'The clinic Dispensary?'

'Right on! We found a fingerprint on the syringe.

He'd had to take his glove off to use it.'

'As simple as that? What about access?'

'Well,' Rootham was still shaking with delight at his own success, 'I reckon something funny was going on at the clinic. That fruity matron and the little nurse must have been up to something that kept them off the corridors. Could be something for the drug squad? Anyway, he broke down immediately. Said he'd walked straight in and did it. Claims his aunt begged him to put her out of her misery.'

'I suppose it's *just* possible.'

'Still murder, though.'

'Oh, quite.' Proby didn't like admitting to himself that he was angry at how the case had been solved so swiftly and comprehensively without him. He'd only been out of action for a few hours, for God's sake! Couldn't Rootham have waited? Surely he didn't think Proby would be refused bail? 'Good work, Ted. Well done.'

'Thank you, sir. It was you who spotted it, though.' Proby glowered at him. Was he being patronized by his own Sergeant?

'My darling!' Sheila was back, this time with a plastic cup.

'Is that whisky?'

'It certainly is.'

'Drinking on duty?' It was the Chief Constable, his narrow face creased with unaccustomed bonhomie. 'Your very good health! I'd like you to take a week's holiday.' He caught sight of Sheila, and his eyes strayed over her. 'It's Mrs Proby, isn't it?' She shook his hand with a modest smile. 'Your husband's a great man,' he said, trying hard not to leer.

'I know,' she said demurely. He really wasn't her type at all. 'But I'll not get him on holiday till he's caught the missing driver.'

'If Ted leaves him long enough for me,' grumbled Proby with a wink at Rootham.

'Good, good.' The Chief Constable felt he had done his bit and more. He could see his chauffeur standing by the door, glowering at the noisy throng. It would be a kindness to get the poor man back to his Daimler and away from all this. 'Keep me in touch.' He hurried away.

Once back in the Incident Room off Jewgate, Proby, Rootham and Mrs Sentance settled down round his desk which was piled high with all the accumulated reports, computer-sheets and other evidence relating to the missing man. Predictably, Braithwaite and Oates had rung through from Tadcaster to say the 'sighting' was yet another case of mistaken identity. The 'fugitive', a door-to-door salesman in encyclopedias, was threatening an action for wrongful arrest – in other words, situation normal!

'What exactly have we got?' said Proby, lighting one of Rootham's cigarettes.

'Well.' Mrs Sentance, who was very experi-

enced in Incident Room technique, had already
analysed the records several times. 'We know his
name, Jack Holland, and we have three separate
photographs, though none showing him with his
beard.'

'He may have shaved it off by now,'
muttered Rootham.

'Or dyed it,' said Proby.

'We're pretty sure he was wounded, maybe
quite seriously, and no hospital or doctor has
reported anything suspicious.'

'Have we kept up the surveillance on the
dodgy doctors?'

She nodded. 'Round-the-clock, and we've
been tapping their telephones since we got
Home Office clearance this morning. Ditto all
known relatives and contacts.'

'Who was the shady doctor at the Hampton
Clinic? We spotted Alf Grimshaw parked across
the road.'

'Hmm.' She had to check through her
notes. 'Dr Gresham, the Medical Director.'

'Really?' Proby was intrigued. 'What else?'

'I've prepared a map. It shows a radius of
fifteen miles from the post office, about the
range he might have covered if they had a back-
up car before we got the road blocks all in place.
You remember there were no vehicles reported
stolen in that time.'

'Doesn't seem likely though, does it?'

'You never know.'

'No. What's this inner ring? I see, that's the three-mile radius – how far he might have got on foot. Let's see… Tenby to the north, round through Claxby, the Bretton crossroads, and then down through Lodden Moor. Lot of woods. It could take months to comb that lot.

'Have you considered he might be dead?' Mrs Sentance said lightly.

Proby massaged his chin, then nodded. 'Yes,' he said. 'We can't exclude that possibility. But I reckon someone's taken him in.'

'A local?'

'Why not?' She pursed her lips. 'I'll tell you what,' he continued. 'Do me a graphic on the locations of other unsolved post office jobs in the area. Let's see what we're looking at. And,' he added, 'make a list of all unusual features, anything at all, in the past fortnight and get the whole lot on the computer. Now, what else do we know about Holland?'

'We know his regiment,' said Rootham, 'and we know where he got his weapon, or rather we know who made it.'

'Exactly. So get the lads digging. I want all the info on his squad, everyone who served with him at close quarters, everything on those gun salesmen. Get the whole caboodle on the computer and let the electronics do some work for a change.'

'Right.' The other two rose obediently, leaving Proby to savour his cigarette in peace.

What a day! Yes, he'd killed four people, five if you counted James Creasey. First there'd been the crazy tramp who'd gone after him with an axe when he was first on the beat. He hadn't meant to kill him, but the man's neck had snapped during the struggle. Within a week, he'd been involved in a major incident with Irish terrorists, which left his Inspector and seven others dead, including the two men he'd had to shoot at close quarters. And the woman? He had no difficulty in recalling Amy Todd. She'd pulled a gun on him when he went to deal with a routine domestic dispute. Would she have killed him? There was no way of knowing, but he hadn't waited to find out. As he pleaded with her to put the gun down, she'd pulled back the hammer and to distract her aim, he'd flung a kitchen knife at her while ducking to his left. A lucky shot? An unlucky shot? Either way, she'd died, right there, in front of her screaming children. What other job placed you in situations like that? The then Chief Constable hadn't liked it, but Proby had been promoted all the same. And he'd been in the same job ever since.

He stood up. 'I'm going home,' he said. 'Ring me as soon as you get anything. Don't forget,' he wagged his finger at Mrs Sentance who was poring over her computer screen. 'Anything at all. I want to know.' It was time to be alone with Sheila.

Chapter 25

They were lying among the wreckage of their sheets, both exhausted, when the call came.

'Sorry, sir.' It was Rootham. 'Julie Dart rang in.'

'And?' Julie had once worked on his squad, a beautiful young woman who'd risked her life to help him solve a case. And Proby, to protect his fragile marriage, had turned away from her just when she had most needed his support. He still felt guilty about her, and, as with most people, guilt made him even more grumpy.

'She didn't say. But she did say it was important. Something about a rape. They're over at the Gower Street station.'

'I'm on my way.'

In the corner of the interview room, a slim young woman was leaning against the wall, her head drooping, while he could see Julie, sat patiently at a little wooden desk, watching her closely. He was about to tap on the door when he heard the girl's voice, low and indistinct through the half-open window. Surely… yes, it was Hannah Grant, the pretty young nurse from the clinic! 'And then he made me…' Angry tears were pouring down her face unchecked. Julie was crying too. She looked up, saw Proby and shook her head violently at him. He withdrew into the shadows and waited.

Eventually she came out, wiping her nose and glowered up at him: 'Well!'

He was a man. Any man at such a time becomes the enemy. He knew about it all too well – the vicissitudes of the Rape Support Squad. He managed to stop himself from touching her, from precipitating a furious reaction. 'Suspect?'

'In Room Seven.' She handed him her casenotes, and turned bitterly away. Whatever she had thought was important enough to drag him in for, he was evidently going to have to find out for himself. He walked slowly down the corridor, remembering his way from when he had been stationed here in the early eighties, passed through a hallway and looked into a bare window-less room, where a burly man was sitting smoking, with a uniformed constable beside him filling in forms. Seeing Proby, he raised a cheery hand. It was Doctor Gresham.

'Hi there!' He was obviously drunk.

Proby sat down, and the constable switched on the tape recorder. 'Interview commencement timed at 22.37 hours. He's been cautioned?' The constable nodded, his face devoid of expression.

Gresham chuckled. 'We've done all that,' he said, wheezing. 'With that fancy bit out there.'

'I'd just like to go through it again.'

'You got off then.' Proby shrugged. It was too much to have expected that Gresham hadn't been following the case. 'Nice work!'

'I'd like to have your version of what happened,' said Proby, ignoring Gresham's leering wink.

'We were celebrating.'

'Celebrating?'

'Yes. The arrest of that poncy nephew. Lifted a cloud from the Clinic, I can tell you.'

Proby glanced at the notes. 'You asked Miss Grant to come to your office?'

'That's right.'

'To check some forms?'

Gresham grinned. 'I had to give her some kind of cover, didn't I?'

'What happened then?'

'We had a drink.'

'You drank....?'

'Vodka. Top stuff. Polish. Cleans your tonsils.'

'Did Miss Grant have some?'

'No! She wanted a Diet Coke. Is it likely I'd have that stuff on tap?'

'What then?'

'I knew what she wanted. We started messing around.'

Proby consulted the notes. 'You grabbed her from behind?'

'A cuddle.'

'Threw her on the floor?'

'Have you ever tried getting it up on a Habitat desk?'

'What's that scratch on your neck?' It was livid and red, and at least eight inches long.

Again the simpering chuckle. 'Little spit-fire!'

'She says you raped her.'

'Ridiculous! She loved it.'

'Why did you have to hit her on the face?'

'Oh. Inspector! What a sheltered life you must lead. The buffetings of passion? The strokes of desire? You should see what she did to my chest!'

'You'll be examined in due course.'

'She loved every minute of it.'

'She says not.'

'She'll change her tune when she's calmed down.'

Proby stared at him. 'What makes you so sure?'

Gresham wagged his head and assumed a conceited smirk. 'Because she knows I know. Dirty little dyke! She wanted it all right. Take my word for it.'

'You'll be examined by the doctor here, and then charged,' said Proby, deciding that he'd had enough. 'Rape and buggery.' Why on earth had Julie dragged him away from his rest for such an unsavoury case? It was none of his business. 'Interview ending timed at 22.49 hours.' He switched off the recorder.

'Can I have a word in private?' Gresham suddenly seemed to have sobered up.

Proby nodded at the constable, who, after a moment's hesitation, picked up the recorder and left the room. 'Well?'

'I'll do a deal.'

Proby frowned. 'A deal?'

'I can help you with something more important.' More important than a violent rape? Proby tried to keep the anger out of his eyes. 'The missing post Office robber? Remember him?'

'Yes?'

'I'll do a deal.'

'I don't quite understand.'

'Yes, you do. I tell you where he is, if you drop these charges. I'd never be convicted. She was screwing that old Colonel *and* my Matron as well as a few more besides. What's a few bruises beside character evidence like that?' He was serious.

Proby rubbed the back of his neck. That Matron? Colonel Bridgeman? Well, why not? He asked himself. Why shouldn't the old boy have a good time? Certainly no one was likely to charge him with rape.

'If you know where Jack Holland is hiding, you're committing a very serious offence indeed in concealing that evidence from the police. You could, and would, be charged as an accessory to murder.'

'I'm not saying I know for sure,' said Gresham with a cunning smile. 'But if you were to offer that as the price for dropping these absurd charges, why then, I'd have to do my best to give you the answer, wouldn't I?'

'Did you mention this to Detective Sergeant Dart?'

'That blonde number?'

'Yes.' What was the point in arguing?

'I certainly did. Off the record.'

'I don't do deals like that,' said Proby, who was increasingly feeling the need to strike the man. And why not? He looked round.

Julie, her face a blank, was standing in the doorway. Unexpectedly, she smiled and shook her head. 'The doctor's ready for him now,' she said. 'Let's talk.'

Chapter 26

'He's got a point.' Julie was staring furiously into her mug of tea. 'She admits she was playing the field a bit.'

'So what?' They seemed to have reversed their natural roles. 'Of course he must be charged.'

'And lose the chance of catching Holland?'

'I can't believe you're saying this, Julie. She's a nice young woman. She didn't deserve whatever happened tonight.'

'You're only saying that because she's pretty. If she was fifteen stone with a wall-eye, you'd say she might have led him on. You fancy her, that's all.' He shrugged. It was partly true. 'You used to fancy me.'

'You're a very fine police officer, and a very beautiful woman. But I'm married.'

'Does your wife know that?'

'If you mean has she had affairs, then yes, she has. As you very well know. But I haven't come here to rake up the past.' He looked at her and sighed. 'Let's get back to Nurse Grant. From your notes, it sounds as if you've got ample corroborative evidence. And that scratch on his neck. It must be half an inch deep.'

'She's terrified of going into court.'

'Because of dear old Colonel Bridgeman?'

'No,' she said flatly, 'because of Barbara Reid.'

'The Matron?'

'Yes.' Their eyes met. 'Says it would kill her parents.'

'Nowadays!'

'That's what she says.'

'She'd rather let a dangerous rapist escape scot-free than embarrass herself?'

'She wouldn't be the first.'

'We could still get him on buggery.'

'And crucify her? They'd be bound to *subpoena* her, for mitigation.'

'I want him put away.'

'What about Holland?'

He nodded. 'Actually,' he said, 'it's my guess he's dead or on his last legs. I doubt he's going anywhere. If Gresham knows where he is, he must have been out to see him before we put him under surveillance yesterday lunchtime. Holland comes a lot lower on my list than the dirty doctor.'

'So where does that leave me?'

Proby finished his coffee and stood up. 'Book him,' he said decisively, 'and get the prosecution to offer a deal once he's got a lawyer. They could offer to drop the second charge in return for a guilty plea. That way he'd probably get away with four years, maybe even less. He needs to be put inside.'

'Will I see you again?'

'I hope so.' An insincere smile, and he was gone.

'Guess what?'

'I'm too tired to guess.' He'd gone back via the Incident Room to see what progress Mrs Sentance had made, and to bring her up-to-date with Gresham's involvement.

'We've found a common link.'

'Oh yes?'

'Remember a Mr George Lubbock?'

'Guy at the armament firm?'

'That's him. Look what the computer's given us.' Proby took the sheet. 'He's got a twenty-three per cent holding in that company. But what's more interesting is that he owns forty per cent of Lodden Investments.'

'And?' It meant nothing.

'Lodden Investments hold the mortgage on the Hampton Clinic.

'Oh?'

'There's more.' put in Rootham eagerly. 'They also own most of what's left of the Lodsworth Castle estate. Lubbock is Lord Lodden's nephew. And...'

'You mean?'

Rootham stared at him. It wasn't like Proby to be slow on the uptake. 'According to the computer,' he said, 'the man, whose company made the murder weapon, also has a financial hold over the doctor who admits to knowing more than he should about where Holland is, *and* owns, or more or less owns, a big estate just where we think Holland's hiding! What more do you want?'

'Got it,' said Proby, his fatigue suddenly gone.

'Lodsworth lies within our inner circle, right?'

'Right.'

'We'll move in at dawn.' Proby reached for the telephone. 'Find me a map, will you?'

Chapter 27

Seven-thirty in the morning, and even the pheasants were only half-awake as they thronged the clearing by the keeper's hut, pecking at the straw while waiting for their morning corn, that treacherous breakfast which both offered them life-giving sustenance and kept them conveniently close to the rising ground from which they would shortly be encouraged to fly over the tall beeches to their deaths.

Proby, bleary-eyed, blew his nose impatiently while Rootham fiddled with his radiophone. 'Everyone in position?'

'I think so.'

Proby drew his revolver. 'Tell them to start, and to keep that effing helicopter out of earshot this time until I say so.'

There were eight buildings marked on the map: the ruined castle with its stables, four cottages, a farmhouse, a dovecote and a Gothic temple. All lay within the old estate wall, a battered and ivy-enveloped heap of stones which ran for nearly five miles in a circle enclosing close on eight hundred acres of woods as well as a few small fields. The approach roads had been sealed off since midnight, with an armed outpost set up by the mainline railway track. A watery sun had begun to emerge twenty minutes ago, and now it was light enough to search.

Oates's team was moving north from the Blayburgh road, starting with the farmhouse, ostensibly inhabited by an elderly tenant and his three sons. Allan's men were fanned out along the main line, beating the woods westwards and halting when they reached the two gamekeepers' cottages on the back drive. Braithwaite was starting with the lodge on the main Hampton road, while Proby, with Rootham and another twelve men in tow, was starting with the two abandoned cottages on the northern boundary, which were, by general consent, the most likely places to hide, before moving on to the castle itself. They had managed to assemble seventy men altogether, from three surrounding counties, more than half of them armed.

The two cottages sat beyond the clearing, low dirty single-storey buildings with sagging roofs and blind windows. The ground around them was open, and whoever approached them, from any angle, would present an easy target from within.

'Cover me!' Ducking low, Proby sprinted across the open ground and flung himself at the right-hand door. It splintered with a satisfying crack and he, tumbled through the debris onto a pile of old sacks. There were cobwebs everywhere, and the sharp smell of birdlime. What with the dust and the droppings, it was clear that no foot had disturbed these floors for at least a year. He could hear one of the Castlewick men axeing his way through the back window, and then Rootham shouted out that the second house was clear.

They spread out again, moving slowly, and methodically, checking the undergrowth to the background of intermittent dull murmuring from pigeons and sudden shrill squeaks from the smaller birds. Once Proby caught the unmistakable reek of a dog fox, and once a shower of twigs betrayed the presence of an angry squirrel. Now he was on one of the forest paths, a cool amber tunnel, muffled by the fallen leaves. To his right he saw, suddenly, a vast and mysterious monolith, rearing up thirty feet, and highlighted as if miraculously by a brilliant miasma of light. It had no particular shape, and the sheen of the massive stone, when he reached it, came from its composition of minute crystals rather than from any human interference. A twisted metal plaque proclaimed that this stone had been erected in 1774 in loving memory of Emmeline, Lady Lodden.

Further on they found the remains of a hermit's cave, a ramshackle conglomeration of boulders with some half-hearted shellwork and the remains of a mosaic floor. Ahead, on an earth mound, he could just make out what had obviously once been the Gothic temple of the map, now just a single arched doorway, with half a brick wall behind. More ruins! These woods were studded with the ineffectual attempts of people trying to build and maintain a roof over their heads.

'Look!' He nearly jumped. Rootham had crept up behind him and was pointing down another narrow line of trees. There was a glitter of water in the distance, but nearer, to the left, stood a squat round tower with a steep slate roof.

'What's that?'

Rootham consulted the waterproofed map. 'The dovecote.' Without waiting for Proby's reply, he strode off down the ride.

'Wait!' But Rootham had already halted, and half-turned his head. 'What is it?'

Rootham sniffed. 'Something funny. Someone's been here.' The low wooden door was apparently locked. 'Who's got the axe?'

'This'll do it.' One of the uniformed men was carrying a crowbar.

Rootham's radio suddenly crackled. 'What?' he said. 'Oh?'

'Well?' Proby was staring at the ground.

'Keepers' houses clear. Ditto the front lodge and the farm. Some very hysterical women, though.'

'We'll clear this, and move in on the Castle.' The policeman struck the lock a heavy blow which resounded among the trees like a pistol shot. The woodwork cracked but held.

'Again.'

The man swung back the bar and put his shoulders into another blow which sent chips of stonework spinning across the ground, while the door sagged on its one remaining hinge. Rootham kicked it in and ducked inside. Proby followed.

'Phew!' Although ventilated by four hatches high up on the walls, the air inside was putrid with a stifling stink of decay. Gradually their eyes grew accustomed to the half-light, and then they saw him, a slumped figure slewed over face-down in the corner.

'Police!' said Rootham, his gun stretched out and ready to fire.

'There's no point,' said Proby gently and turned away. But as he did, the figure moved. His back quivered and Rootham, seeing the movement out of the corner of his eye, whirled and ran at him, pulling the man's shoulder round with one hand as he raised the other to strike. Except the shoulder came away in his hand. And then he saw the face, with its bones bare and the flesh alive with coiling satiated maggots, twisting and turning in the ecstasy of repletion. One eye was glazed but intact, the other bulged with one gross sluggish worm, which curled up at him, squeezing itself through the empty socket. He tried to speak, but felt himself vomiting over the dreadful bubbling mass.

Chapter 28

'Lord Lodden?'

'Yes?' The poor old man had woken to find his rural haven swarming with armed men and flashing lights. Pulling his tattered dressing-gown around him, he had eventually made himself go out into the chilly morning to enquire how he might help these strange interlopers.

'We'd like you to come into Hampton to answer some questions.'

To Hampton? Into the *city*? How many years had it been? 'Delighted, my dear fellow. And you are?'

'Inspector Proby, Hampton CID.'

'I've got the chickens to feed, you know.'

'I'll make sure someone takes care of them.'

'And the cat?' His feet were bare, the yellowed toenails so long that they curled pitifully in upon themselves.

'And the cat, sir.' The confused old man hobbled back across the cobbles and through the green door to look for his clothes. 'Have they picked up Lubbock?'

'Ten minutes ago. He came without any trouble.'

'That's a relief. I wouldn't have liked to storm that factory! Did you recognize him?'

Rootham stared. 'Who?'

'Lord Lodden.'

'No. Should I have?'

'You've seen his picture recently.'

'His picture?' Rootham screwed up his eyes in thought, then smiled. '*Colonel of the Regiment*!'

'And I bet you his nephew served in it too. He had the lot, didn't he? Ready recruits from the family regiment, top of the range fire-power, and a perfect hiding-place. Even a tame doctor. I bet the old boy never had the faintest idea what was going on.'

'But… will we convict Lubbock?'

'I doubt it. Plenty of circumstantial evidence, but unless forensic come up with something, what is there? The men are all dead. Anyone could hide in a wood.'

'But… the locked door?'

Proby nodded. 'That's our best bet. If we haven't knocked it about too much to prove that it was locked.'

'Sir!'

'What?'

'Down here!' They hurried round the side of the ruin and down the steps towards the Castle cellars. 'Inside.'

The old coal train rails ran down a slight incline to where a massive pair of wooden doors were now standing open. Inside, towering over the debris of sixty years' clutter, stood a small diesel-powered goods train, with massive pneu-

matic tyres mounted awkwardly instead of its
conventional wheels, which were propped out of
the way against the wall. Lying casually on the
driver's seat was a shiny new Fletcher and
Houston 9 mm with a box of ammunition beside
it.

'Let's see him talk his way out of this,' said
Rootham with relish. 'He's as guilty as…'

'As I was?' murmured Proby with a thin
smile. 'There's a long chain of events between a
crime and its proof. I think yes, I'll see him in my
office.'

'You've been cautioned?'

Lubbock nodded, and leaned back in his
chair with his friendly smile. Proby had sent out
for some tea, and had even offered him the cigar
he'd been given at last Christmas's Divisional
Jamboree. 'I certainly have!'

'And you don't want a lawyer present?'

Lubbock shook his head. 'Not at the prices
those fellows charge nowadays. An arm and a leg,
I'm telling you!'

Proby rose and crossed to the window.
Outside, in the carpark, and in the children's
playground beyond, the wind was whisking the
last leaves into a frenzy, weird planing discs of
brown-and-yellow decay, skimming and spiralling
through the frosty air. A solitary child, her head
hung low, was kicking at some twigs, while the
small white dog, attached to her by a piece of

string, dug furiously at a molehill. Would she be the same age as Debbie, the little girl in the adoption photograph, the one who needed a '*forever*' family?

'We've found Holland,' he said.

'Holland?'

'Yes,' snapped Rootham, who had been lounging against the back wall. 'Remember him? Jack Holland? He was a corporal in your platoon in Londonderry, summer 1981.

'Why, yes! Jack Holland. I believe I do remember him. Big man, not very bright. He'd never make sergeant.'

'He was found dead,' said Proby. 'Had been for several days. Locked in a building at Lodsworth.'

Lubbock raised his eyebrows. Everything about him was careful; the meticulously knotted silk tie, the crisp white shirt, the expensively tailored suit of blue mohair. One of life's winners, with his plump pink cheeks and sleek black hair, brushed back to reveal a large and unlined forehead. Really, he didn't appear to have a care in the world. 'My uncle's estate?'

'Which you run for him!'

'Well,' he spread out his hands, 'up to a point.'

'Are you denying that you handle all the administration?'

'No,' he grinned, showing perfect teeth. 'But most of that's done through the office. I go there, what, once a week at most, just to check my uncle's okay, and for a chat with Greg Toler. He's Head Keeper, you know.'

Proby nodded. 'We have Mr Toler here now.'

'Toler? Here?' He let out an explosion of laughter. 'I hope you won't keep the poor chap locked up too long. He hates cities. Very much a country chap. Like me.'

Proby strolled back to the window. The wind had dropped, and the leaves lay dead. The child had gone too. It would soon be winter. Where would Debbie be then? 'Let me lay it out for you,' he said. 'The three dead men were all in your platoon in Ulster. The two highly restricted weapons and their ammunition were supplied by your company. The body of Holland was found locked in a building on an estate which you administer and partly own.'

'Hmm.' Lubbock sipped his tea. 'All rather circumstantial, isn't it?'

'We also,' said Proby, 'found a train in the Castle cellars.'

'A train?' He was laughing at them.

'It appears to have been adapted to run on rough ground instead of railway tracks. Presumably by Gilbert who was an expert engineer.'

Lubbock allowed himself a broad smile. 'Is that a *question*, Inspector?'

Proby shook his head. 'We haven't established exactly what it was intended for, but there is no doubt it caused the railway accident last Saturday, and there will be charges arising from that as well.'

'Gracious!' Lubbock examined his nails. 'I do wish I could help you. I really do.'

'Well.' said Proby, sitting down and deliberately matching his prey's nonchalant pose, 'you could help me by providing an explanation of these circumstances, which do not involve you.'

Lubbock screwed up his eyes and bit his lower lip as if engaging in a monumental exercise of deduction. At last, he shook his head. 'Looks bad for Uncle Henry,' he said, as if reluctantly.

'You can't be serious!' Rootham lunged forward. 'That harmless old man. He hardly knows what day it is.'

Lubbock sighed. 'Uncle Henry is a bit of a fraud, I'm afraid. He rather cultivates the image of helpless old codger, but he still presides perfectly well at regimental dinners, shoots two days a week, and pops up to London most months.'

'So why would he want to get involved in post office robberies?'

'Why would I, for that matter?' drawled Lubbock. 'I've no doubt you'll examine all the bank records. You'll find that money is not one of my immediate necessities.' He leaned back in his chair, and stretched out his arms. 'I don't suppose you'd run to a cheese sandwich?'

Proby beamed at him. 'Certainly,' he said.

'I'm quite hungry myself Ted! Get us four rounds of cheese…'

'With mustard!' put in Lubbock.

'…With mustard. And a couple of bottles of lager. Skol do?'

Lubbock pulled a face. 'I expect it'll have to. But Carlsberg if they've got it. Or Löwenbräu.'

'Do what you can, Ted.' Proby saw Rootham's constipated expression and winked. 'So tell me about this train?'

'You tell me, Inspector. It sounds very amusing.'

'My theory is that it was intended to do just what it did. Appear on the same track out of the blue, so that a collision seemed imminent. The real train would then brake so violently that it would come adrift.'

'Wouldn't that be dangerous? What if the train-driver was dozing and it didn't stop?'

'Ah! But this contraption isn't really running on the tracks, it just appears to. It can nip off out of the way, and it doesn't leave traces where it's been, down through the woods and so on. Rather an ingenious idea.' He shot a sudden glance at Lubbock, but if he had hoped for some sign of pride, some acknowledgement of the compliment, he was disappointed. Lubbock was frowning, as if in bewilderment.

'But why,' he said, 'would anyone want to cause a train to crash?'

'Same principle as eighteenth-century

wreckers, I expect,' said Proby. 'Particularly as the Royal Mint uses that line once a month.'

'*The Royal Mint?* You mean *gold?*' He was overacting now, an encouraging sign.

'I don't think it's a secret.' said Proby affably. 'There are regular movements of bullion from the Mount Webster vaults. Between you and me, I reckon the post office jobs were just to collect enough cash to finance the big one. You know, pay the middle men up-front, that sort of thing.'

'Why are you telling me all this?' asked Lubbock slowly.

'Because you know it anyway,' said Proby, adding, for the benefit of the recording, 'Interview suspended 12.32 hours. I've got a couple of other things to do. I'll come back to share those sandwiches with you.'

'I'll look forward to that,' said Lubbock cheerfully, and, taking a slim paperback out of his pocket, he settled himself more comfortably and began to read, under the stolid, but incredulous, stare of the uniformed constable sitting in the corner by the radiator.

Proby only had to walk four doors down the corridor to the room where Dr Gresham, his face shiny with sweat, was slumped in a chair, being questioned by Allan and Oates. Beside him sat his solicitor.

'Detective Inspector Proby has just entered

the room,' declaimed the latter, rising and offering his seat to his superior, as the solicitor introduced herself as Miss Jane Lopes, a junior partner in the local firm of Donaldson, Smith, Coates and Dawson.

'Good morning, Doctor.' Gresham just looked at him. 'How's the head?'

'Not good.'

'How about some coffee?'

'No thanks.'

'You know you're going to be charged with rape and buggery.' No reply. 'Miss Lopes here will have told you that you'll get four years if you can show provocation and seven to nine if you can't.' He glanced at the solicitor, who nodded.

'My client will be pleading not guilty to the first charge,' she said, rather halfheartedly.

'Your client,' said Proby, 'is in much deeper water now.'

Doctor and solicitor both looked up sharply. 'How so?' she said anxiously.

'I have a Mr George Lubbock in custody next door. Your client,' said Proby, leafing through his papers as if to check a detail, 'will be charged with being an accessory to the murders of Mary Clark, Edward Moss, Clive Pollock and Police Constable Douglas Hickock, and for knowingly withholding information from the police in the execution of their duty.'

'That's bloody rubbish!' Gresham was on his feet, shouting hoarsely. 'Bloody *rubbish*!'

'You treated Jack Holland on the morning of Tuesday this week…'

'He was dead! He was fucking dead! I didn't know who he was…'

'Lubbock says...'

'Lubbock's a liar.'

'He says he told you it was Jack Holland.'

'It's not true. Lubbock's LYING! He was crawling with *lice* for Christ's sake! I've never seen anything like it, not EVER.' Dr Gresham sat down on his chair again and started to sob.

'So,' Proby turned a fresh page, giving the startled solicitor a long hard stare. 'Let's hear your version, shall we?' The oldest trick. No deductive genius. No inspired insights. Just the usual clichés. It was simply a matter of routine from now on, the slow, dogged drudgery of policework, that paid the mortgage and bought him and Sheila their holiday in the sun.

Soon it would be time to face Lubbock. What had his motivation been, to reject a comfortable privileged life for such violent gambling? A compulsion to plan, to act? Or simple greed? More probably a need for adventure, and in particular for the risk of military adventure. When society trains soldiers, officers and men alike, it trains them to lose the taboo against killing. But having made them killers, was it prudent to cast them out penniless into civilian life, like tigers, hungry and, worse, with a grudge – creatures who had learnt what it was like to inspire terror in others, and to feel and control their own fear?

And for that, seven people had died. Proby felt for his cigarettes. Certainly he wasn't feeling hungry any more.